CONCRETE EVIDENCE

Evan was staring impassively into the mess at his feet when Kelly and Sarah dashed towards him, calling, "Are you all right?"

He didn't respond. His face was grey, speckled with dust. His gaze was fixed. He had retreated into his own private world.

"Evan?"

Kelly's eyes followed Evan's stare. Suddenly, her hand darted to her mouth. Beside her, Sarah screamed at the top of her voice. "No, no!" she cried. The three Keatings were gaping at a body lying among the rubble of the collapsed wall. It was the remains of their mother.

Other titles in the Point Crime series:

POINT CRIME

CONCRETE EVIDENCE

Malcolm Rose

Cover illustration by David Wyatt

SCHOLASTIC INC.

New York Toronto London Auckland Sydney

ISBN 0-590-20358-4

First published in the UK in 1995 by Scholastic Publications Ltd. Text copyright © 1995 by Malcolm Rose. Cover illustration copyright © 1995 by David Wyatt. All rights reserved. Published by Scholastic Inc. POINT is a registered trademark of Scholastic Inc.

12 11 10 9 8 7 6 5 4 3 2 1   5 6 7 8 9/9 0/0

Printed in the U.S.A.   01

First Scholastic printing, April 1995

CONCRETE EVIDENCE

1

Thump! Thump! Thump! Thump!

Kelly looked up from the kitchen sink and smiled. "He'll wear out our view, will Evan, if he keeps that up," she remarked.

Tea towel in hand, Sarah glanced out of the window. "The wall's in a bad way even without our beloved brother's help," she said. "There's a good few cracks already and they're getting wider – subsidence or poor workmanship." She hesitated, then added, "You know who built it, don't you?"

"Yeah," Kelly replied glumly. "Henderson's."

The sisters resumed the washing up in thoughtful silence.

Thump! Thump! Thump!

Six months ago, they could see the industrial

estate from their kitchen window, and hear the traffic and the machines. Not a great view, but at least they'd felt part of the real world. Then their mother lost her long, hard battle over planning permission and, almost overnight it seemed, the extension to the video factory appeared at the bottom of their garden. Now the estate, traffic and machines were hidden behind a bland concrete wall, but it wasn't an improvement, as their mum had anticipated all along. The factory owner's solution to the Keatings' worries had been to paint a giant mural on the concrete monstrosity. Now they had a view of two-dimensional rolling hills and, of course, the goal mouth that Evan had added with an aerosol so that he could practise shooting and ball control.

Evan was the only one who approved of the wall. Every day he spent an hour kicking a ball rhythmically against it. Sometimes he would stop and stare at the mural as if he were sizing it up. No one knew what was going through his mind when he wore that faraway expression, but then the moment would pass and he would resume the clockwork kicking. Volley with the left foot against the wall. Control the rebound on the right thigh. Volley with the right foot. Control the rebound on the left thigh. Volley. *Thump! Thump! Thump!*

Without warning, Kelly shrieked and dropped a clean plate back into the soapy dish-water.

A car, out of control, had ploughed straight through the hedge on the right-hand side of the garden, bounced up on to the lawn and was careering towards Evan and the wall.

"Evan!" the sisters screamed in unison.

A black cat padding across the lawn let out a yowl and sprang out of the way. Less agile, Evan spun round and the football hit him on the back as he dived to one side. The car shot past him and slammed into the concrete hills with a sickening crash.

Glass shattered, metal crumpled, shrapnel flew. The front end of the car was crushed. The engine stalled. A second or two later, part of the wall leaned, tottered as if it were trying to keep its balance, and then collapsed. Great chunks of concrete fell on to the grass and the car's bonnet in an unearthly clatter.

When the dust settled, the lawn was littered with fragments of painted poplars, people and hillside. The car was smothered with rubble and the gap in the wall revealed machines that churned out videos by the hundreds.

Evan was staring impassively into the mess at his feet when Kelly and Sarah dashed towards him, calling, "Are you all right?"

He didn't respond. His face was grey, speckled with dust. His gaze was fixed. He had retreated into his own private world.

"Evan?"

Kelly's eyes followed Evan's stare. Suddenly, her hand darted to her mouth. Beside her, Sarah screamed at the top of her voice. "No, no!" she cried. The three Keatings were gaping at a body lying among the rubble of the collapsed wall. It was the remains of their mother.

Her legs were still encased in concrete but the rest of her body had broken free of its cruel cage, like a life-size statue emerging from its mould. Much of her clothing had stuck to the concrete and ripped away from the body. Her skin was as grey as parchment, and lay like a taut shroud over prominent bones; her hair was like straw and her eyes were sunken and black. The remains had begun to decay and the putrid smell was revolting. Even so, they recognized their mother – their mother who, just over five months ago, was supposed to have run off with another man. Now misshapen, she lay on the ground and hundreds of woodlice, made homeless by the collapse of the wall, crawled all over her.

The doors of the car creaked open and the two young joyriders staggered out. Smiling, obviously on a high, one chirped, "Fantastic! They build these cars well. Stronger than concrete."

"Great things, crumple zones," the other replied.

When they saw that they weren't alone in the garden, they were surprised – even disappointed –

not to be the centre of attention. Then they saw the body and they turned and fled, unnoticed by the Keatings.

Sarah clutched her sister, using Kelly's shoulder to muffle her uncontrollable sobs. Neither sister had seen a dead body before, and now they had to confront not just the hideous sight of death but their own mother's corpse.

Evan wiped his face with the sleeve of his green jumper, picked up the football, turned his back on the relic of his mother and walked away in silence.

Eventually, Kelly separated herself from Sarah. "Come on," she said. "Let's go in. We can't do anything for her out here, that's for sure. We'd better call Dad – and the police."

2

"It's what's known in the trade as a cock-up," Detective Chief Inspector Neil Tatton said to his new sergeant as they sped towards the Keatings' house. He used flippancy to cover up his annoyance. His last case remained unsolved and now a mistake in an old inquiry had come back to plague him. He wasn't looking forward to the inevitable dressing down from the Superintendent. He sighed and opened Mrs Keating's file on his knee.

"October, last year. Mrs Barbara Keating. Husband reported her missing on the morning of Saturday the fourteenth. She never came home after work on the Friday. In door-to-door checks, some local bobby with a photo found a restaurant owner, at The Seafood Spree, who identified her.

She'd taken an early evening meal in his place — with a mystery man. We christened him Mr Fish. Keating and Mr Fish were the first customers in the restaurant that night, so the owner remembered them quite well. A lovers' tryst, he thought. Scheming going on between them. Nervous and excited, he said they were. All lovey-dovey too, like a couple of teenagers planning to elope. That was the last sighting."

He turned over a page then continued, "The husband, Clive Keating, didn't admit to knowing his wife was being unfaithful, but the kids knew all right. Kelly, Sarah and Evan. Ages of . . . let's see . . . eighteen, sixteen and fifteen. The lad was big for his age — and a bit of a screwball, if I remember rightly. As slippery as a fish himself, but he virtually admitted that he knew his mum had got herself a bit on the side. He was smarting over it, I reckoned at the time. He said he'd had an argument with her on the Friday morning. 'You're breaking up the family so you don't love me any more' — that sort of thing. Then she vamoosed. It looked straightforward," the detective said as he closed the file, "especially backed by the best piece of evidence available at the time."

"What was that?" Detective Sergeant Vicky McCormick asked.

"Think about it," DCI Tatton replied unhelpfully. The sergeant took a right turn then glanced triumphantly at her passenger. "No body," she concluded.

"Bingo! If Keating knew about the lover and did his wife in or if the kid, Evan, got carried away, there'd be a body. Crimes of passion always provide a body."

"But now we have one," Vicky murmured.

"Right. An open and shut case is open again, and I think we can assume it's a murder inquiry."

"Want me to jump the lights, Neil?" she asked as she neared a crossroads.

"No. The body's not going anywhere. It'll wait for us."

As she brought the car to a standstill at the red light, Vicky inquired, "Ever identify Mr Fish?"

"No," Neil answered. "They didn't book the table in his name. It was early enough in the evening to just drop in."

"How about payment? A cheque or Visa sales voucher with Mr Fish's real name and signature?"

"Unfortunately not," he grumbled. "Paid in cash. They didn't eat much. Not a big bill."

"I thought everyone paid by plastic these days," Vicky commented, taking a left turn past the canal. "Still, my husband hasn't taken me to a decent restaurant for so long, I wouldn't know." Her voice was deep, almost like a man's.

"The best we got out of the restaurant owner – Daniel Perriman – was a description. And that was a bit vague, a bit average. You know: white, average height, average mousy hair, no distinguishing features. Could have been me or thousands of others. I think the owner paid more attention to Barbara Keating. They left together, Keating and Mr Fish."

"Last person to see her alive, possibly."

"Yes. I'd quite like to speak to our Mr Fish," Neil said, in a tone overflowing with understatement.

When they arrived, the scene-of-the-crime team was crawling all over the place. Two officers with a very long tape measure were noting the distances between the road, the smashed hedge and the wall. From their measurements, a detailed plan of the area would be constructed later. Some other workers were shoring up the stricken part of the wall, making the building safe. Picking his way through the debris towards the body, DCI Tatton stopped by the car and watched a young forensic scientist dusting the surfaces for fingerprints.

"What are you doing that for?" he barked.

"The boss said make a thorough job of it."

"Well, I'm the governor now. And I imagine the victim was already dead when the car hit the wall. The rest of us are after a murderer, you know, not a joyrider. Your time would be better spent tracing the car's owner so he can give his insurers the bad news."

"Yes, sir."

DCI Tatton barely glanced at the victim. He had always found examining bodies distasteful. Besides, his job was to police the living, not to take care of the dead. Instead, he asked the pathologist, "What have you got for me?"

"Not a lot. Female. About forty years old. Partly mummified, partly decomposed. From the inside. Consistent with being buried in the wall for some months."

"The daughter called us," Tatton said. "We know who the victim is. And building records will tell me when she was dunked in concrete. Friday 13th October last year would be my guess. In the dark, probably. So are you going to give me anything that I don't already know?"

Vicky had not known Neil Tatton for long, so she wasn't familiar with his character and moods, but this morning the signs of irritation were hardly subtle. Clearly, she thought, this case was giving him the creeps. Trying to put the pathologist in a better frame of mind, she interjected, "Any obvious cause of death?"

He shrugged. "No sign of physical damage as far as I can see. No blood stains, no broken bones."

"She wasn't shot, knifed or battered, then," Neil declared. "Strangulation?"

"This isn't a fresh body, Tatton. I can't look for bruising, you know. The skin's like leather and covered in concrete in places," he replied. "The neck's intact, though – I can tell you that. Maybe a closer examination in the lab will reveal something."

With a grimace on her face, Vicky asked, "Was she alive, do you think, when she went into the concrete?" It wasn't a pleasant thought.

"I don't think so," the pathologist answered. "The inside of the mouth and nose are free of concrete so she didn't gasp for air. She was probably dead or unconscious."

Sergeant McCormick paused then added, "Found her bag yet?"

"Don't ask me. I'm a bodies man, not a handbag man." He called to one of his colleagues who shouted back, "No. Not yet."

In turn, Vicky yelled, "Keep looking. With women there's always a bag – somewhere."

"Okay. That's all for now," Tatton muttered. Turning to Vicky, he said, "Come on. We'll get on with our job and let these guys get on with theirs. We'll get their report soon enough." Heading towards the house, he asked, "Tell me, Sergeant McCormick, what do you make of this method of disposing of the body?"

"Typical gangland stuff," Vicky answered. "Perhaps she was mixed up in some organized crime. Drug dealing, possibly. It also tells us that someone didn't want the body to be found."

"Mmm." The Chief Inspector pondered for a

moment. "Could be that our man is simply off his rocker."

"I didn't deduce that the culprit was male," Vicky retorted.

"They're usually male," Tatton replied. "And dumping bodies in concrete is a particularly macho thing to do." Changing the subject, he asked, "Have you decided who we need to interview?"

"I think so."

"Well?"

"The family, obviously. Especially the husband. And the lad, Evan. The building site workers – they'll need to be traced. And the manager of that restaurant."

"Why him?" he asked, obviously testing her.

"We need Mr Fish. Badly. Perhaps we can jog the owner's memory for something else. More information."

"After five and a bit months?"

"I know it's a long shot, but even so . . ."

"Okay. Is that it?"

"No," she responded. "I think we'd better have words with Mr Eric Henderson."

"Henderson?"

She smiled cockily. "Henderson of Henderson's Builders. He got the building contract on this factory, I think."

Hesitating before he knocked on the door to the house, Neil queried, "How do you know that?"

"My so-called better half works there. In one of those rare moments when we actually speak to each other, he told me about this site, I'm sure."

"Henderson, then. And don't look so pleased with yourself, Sergeant. It was hardly great detective work. Just the right connection, that's all."

"Isn't having the right connections one of the hallmarks of a good detective?" she replied.

The Keatings remembered Detective Chief Inspector Tatton. Those few months ago, he was the one who'd broken the news that Mrs Keating had been seen with another man in a restaurant in town. To a different extent, each of the Keatings had resented him for bringing into the open what, in private, they all knew – Mrs Keating was seeing another man. Somehow, once their secret had been announced as a fact by an outsider, they felt more cheapened, sullied and cheated.

While her unfaithfulness had remained unspoken, there was always the chance that it might suddenly stop and there would be nothing to be ashamed of any more. Neil Tatton had shattered that hope. None of the kids could deny that it looked as if their mother had deserted them, but their dad, too proud to admit the truth, had mounted a feeble protest. DCI Tatton was certain. He had told them calmly and clinically why he believed Mrs Keating had run off with another man, and why he was closing the case. He'd seemed eager to finish the business quickly and get on to another, more exciting, case.

Now he sat in front of them again. He still bore the expression of someone who would rather be somewhere else, doing something else. He did not appear to be embarrassed, but he was clearly disgruntled at having to admit to an error.

"I won't ask you lots of questions now," he was saying, "because I know you've had a shock. But I do have to make fresh inquiries, of course. I'll come back tomorrow."

"What for?" Mr Keating mumbled.

"I realize it's difficult for you," Tatton answered, with just a trace of impatience in his tone. "I'll have to ask you all to cast your minds back to October, just before Mrs Keating disappeared."

"Fresh inquiries?" Mr Keating snapped. "What does that mean? Are you now saying she was murdered?"

"I haven't ruled it out," DCI Tatton responded dryly. "The manner in which the body was disposed of suggests murder, I'm afraid."

"Last time," Clive Keating complained, "the lack of body suggested she'd run off. I told you she hadn't. I was right. You made a right old cock-up."

With considerable difficulty, Vicky kept her face straight as her partner objected, "I don't think that's entirely fair, Mr Keating. It was the best interpretation of the evidence at the time. It looked watertight. But now we have a new piece of evidence, so we have to think again. It's a process of refinement and reconsideration till we get to the truth."

"Perhaps you'd better reconsider if there ever *was* another man."

To Kelly, her father seemed rather sad, perhaps even a little desperate. To Sergeant McCormick, it seemed possible that Clive Keating was trying to suggest that he lacked the motive of jealousy. If his wife had never had a lover after all, he would never have had cause to take his revenge. The sorrow and anger in his eyes could be the result of seeing the remains of a loved one but, equally, he could be regretting a crime that had come back to haunt him.

The boy was different. He was handsome but his eyes told her nothing. Behind them there could be a little angel or a little devil, or maybe both. Maybe he was an angel who endured dark moods, periods when the devil would rule.

The two girls appeared to be much less complex. They were genuinely shocked by the find but, as they looked sadly at their father, it was plain to see that their sympathies lay with him, not with their mum. Vicky estimated that they knew they'd lost their mother some time before she even went missing. They looked worldly enough to recognize a mother who was sharing her affections with an outsider. Kelly, the older sister, probably mothered the family now. Vicky knew that the male of the species did not have a monopoly on murder, but she could not regard either sister as a serious suspect.

"I think we'll call a halt to this conversation for now," Tatton said, rising from his chair. "We'll talk again tomorrow when you've all had a bit of time to get over the initial shock. My officers will soon finish in the garden and leave you in peace."

"What about . . . er. . . ?" Sarah uttered. She still couldn't bring herself to mention her mum's corpse.

"They'll remove the body for examination. And they've got in some contractors to take care of the wall. It won't be left unsafe."

"We'll make sure they tidy up," Vicky added, "so you don't have that to worry about as well."

3

Mr Keating ran a small newsagent's shop in the suburbs. It ticked over on sales of magazines, newspapers, cigarettes and confectionery, but would never make the family wealthy. Before her death, Mrs Keating had topped up the family income by working part-time as a secretary at Henderson's Builders. When they weren't at school, the girls would often help in the shop and their brother earned extra pocket money by taking on the newspaper round. It always took the promise of payment to drag Evan out of his permanent state of detachment – the whiff of money acted like smelling salts to him.

The next day, Evan sat alone in his bedroom and the girls whispered nervously to each other while police officers interviewed their dad in the dining room. After a restless night both sisters were on edge.

"How are you?" asked Kelly.

"Rough."

"No sleep? Nor me," Kelly said. "Thinking about Mum."

Shivering, Sarah replied, "Yeah. Horrible." Banishing the unwanted image from her mind, she added, "Now we've got to face the police. What do you think? Will it be all right?"

Both Sarah and Kelly had been questioned by police officers before, almost six months ago, but then it all seemed straightforward – an inquiry, not an inquisition. Now the police were trying to trap a murderer and anyone they interviewed was under suspicion to some extent. That made them feel like crooks under threat of discovery.

"Just tell them what you know," Kelly advised her sister.

"Not much," Sarah replied. "But what if they ask about Dad, or Evan?"

"There's nothing you can do but tell the truth. They'll notice if you try to lie."

"But do you think Dad. . . ?"

"He loved her, Sarah. I'm sure he did."

"So if he found out she was seeing someone else. . . ?"

Kelly shrugged. "I still don't think he'd . . . you know."

Listlessly, Sarah wound a lock of hair round and round a finger. "What about Evan?"

Her sister sighed. "He's a law unto himself. I'm not sure he's got it in him to have a go at anyone, though. At least, I hope not."

"He was upset that day, you know. And he did argue with Mum. Remember? What was that all about?"

"I don't know. He wouldn't say. I'll tell you one thing, though," Kelly said, "I bet the police try to squeeze it out of him."

"They'll be lucky!"

Vicky McCormick sat opposite Mr Keating at the dining table while Neil Tatton skulked round and round them like some subtle parasite. "How would you have described your marriage?" he probed.

"How do you mean?" Mr Keating squirmed.

"Happy, harmonious, troubled, stormy?"

Mr Keating shrugged. "It was like many a twenty-year-old-marriage, I suppose."

"And what's that like?"

"It means rather more respect than passion. We weren't spring chickens."

"I see what you mean," DCI Tatton replied. "A middle-aged marriage."

"Yes."

"So," he asked, looking for once into his suspect's

face, "did either of you try to find passion elsewhere?"

"We've been through all this before!" Mr Keating exploded.

"True. But I wondered if you'd changed your view in the light of this new development."

"No," Clive retorted. "I wasn't aware of my wife seeing anyone else. Despite your evidence, I'm not inclined to believe that she . . . strayed," he said proudly. Even so, a little sweat appeared on his brow, as he sat bolt upright in perfect military posture.

"Mmm." Annoyingly, the detective completed a lap of the dining room before he asked another question. He stopped pacing and inquired, "What about you, Mr Keating?"

"What about me?"

"Did you try to rekindle the flames with someone else?"

Clive Keating was taken aback by the unexpected question. After a split-second pause, he declared, "Certainly not."

"Many men of your age do."

"I've got my hands full with the shop. Even if I'd wanted to, I'd never have time for an affair. Too busy. I was quite happy with my circumstances, I assure you."

Changing tack without warning, Tatton asked, "Run again through your movements on the evening of Friday 13th October."

"I . . . er . . . I was in the shop till closing time."

"When's that?" Sergeant McCormick put in.

"Seven," he answered. "Then I had quite a lot of sorting out to do. I didn't leave the shop till after seven thirty. I got home about eight. Barbara wasn't here so I warmed up a pie or something, and ate."

"Did any regular punters come into the shop? Ones who could confirm that you were there?"

In a weary voice, Clive Keating muttered, "How am I supposed to remember that after five or six months?"

"Okay," Neil Tatton conceded. "Who else was at home when you got back?"

"No one. They were all out. Kelly was off to one of those all-night dance things."

"A rave," Vicky commented.

"Yes," Mr Keating added. "That's it. But I don't know about Sarah and Evan. If you want to know what they were doing, you'll have to ask them."

"We will," the detective replied tersely. "Carry on from the dinner."

"I watched the nine o'clock news, then a film."

"Which film?" asked the sergeant.

Mr Keating grinned. "That's easy. They showed *Friday the Thirteenth*."

Vicky nodded. "Ah, yes. Nearly Hallowe'en as well. Out come the horror films. I wanted to watch that one but . . . I missed it, I'm afraid. It was the one where Donald Pleasance chases a psychopath and Jamie Lee Curtis nearly cops it, wasn't it?"

"No," Clive answered. "It's the cheap rip-off of the film you've got in mind. No big stars, as far as I remember, just blood and gore. Teenagers getting hacked to pieces in a summer camp."

The DCI took control of the questioning again. "BBC or ITV?"

Clive Keating sighed. "I *have* got an IQ above ten, you know. If I was making this up as an alibi, I'd have checked my facts first. So do these tests prove anything?"

"BBC or ITV?" Tatton repeated.

"The film followed the BBC news and there were no adverts."

"Did you notice any activity on the building site that evening?"

"The men were working late by floodlights when I first came in and made the meal. I ate in front of the telly. By the time I washed up, the lights were off. I wouldn't say I saw anything odd."

"When did you wash up?"

"Er . . . after the film. About eleven, I suppose. Eleven thirty at the latest."

"And had the kids returned by then?" asked Vicky.

"Kelly was still out. Sarah and Evan came back just before the end of the film, I think."

"Together?" Neil Tatton queried.

"No, separately."

"Okay," Detective Chief Inspector Tatton announced. "That's enough for now. You can go. But we'd like a word with Evan next. Can you tell him to wait outside till we call him in?"

"Well, Vicky," Neil muttered when they were alone, "what do you think? Did he know his wife was carrying on, or didn't he? And if he knew, would he have killed her for it?"

"Yes, he knew," Vicky replied. "I'm sure he did. But he won't admit it – even to himself. And if he wouldn't admit it to himself, he wouldn't have a reason to take it out on her. If he denied himself the truth about his wife, he had no motive."

"Mmm." Neil pondered on the matter. "Maybe," he added. Then, without warning, he asked her, "What about *your* husband? If he was cheating on you, would you know?"

The Detective Sergeant hesitated. She didn't like the intrusion into her private life but knew that Neil wasn't really interested in it – he was just using it to assist the inquiry. "With this job, I hardly ever see him," she quipped. "Sometimes, I reckon I'd have trouble picking him out in an identity parade. Anyway," she continued, returning to the matter in hand, "what are you getting at? That Keating may have been so preoccupied with his business that the marriage fell apart without him noticing?"

Neil shrugged. "You didn't answer my question."

Abruptly, Vicky replied, "We're investigating the Keatings' marriage, not mine, but I think a husband or wife always knows when their partner's having an affair, even if they're busy or trying to pretend it's not happening. Deep down, they always know."

"Mmm." Neil sat down. After a pause, he asked, "By the way, did he get that stuff about the film right?"

"Yes. And he knew the difference between *Friday the Thirteenth* and *Halloween*," she answered. "That part of his story holds up."

"You must have a good memory for these things."

Vicky smiled. "Bit of a movie buff. Besides, I *did* want to see it, but duty called that night."

"It often does. Too often," Neil remarked. He cleared his throat, then asked, "Have you got kids?"

"No." The sergeant looked a little disappointed.

"So you don't know how an affair would affect the kids?"

"Not first-hand, no."

"Well, the textbook sentiments are jealousy and resentment. That's our Evan, I think. You can expect the children in a broken family to be confused and angry . . . or, like Evan, simmering. They can even blame themselves for the break-up. But one thing's for sure: they don't want to take second place behind an outsider. They feel betrayed, especially when it's the mother who's doing the betraying. And lads tend not to share their feelings. The girls would talk about their troubled home life, but Evan would bottle it up. The question is, just how angry was he? Angry enough?" Neil stood up again sprightly. "Let's try to break down his defences and find out."

Evan bit his nails and fidgeted in his seat as he answered the police officers' questions in monosyllables. He rarely looked into his interrogators' faces.

"Where were you," DCI Tatton queried, "on the night of your mother's disappearance between, say, eight and midnight?"

"How should I know?" Evan muttered. "It was ages ago."

"We know it's difficult," Vicky interjected, using a softly softly approach, "but try to cast your mind back."

"Everyone knows where they were and what they were doing when really big events took place," Neil Tatton added. "For you, there can't have been a much bigger event than your mother's disappearance."

"I was out."

"Out where?"

Evan shrugged. "Walking."

Incredulous, the detective responded, "For four hours on a cold, wet night?" He hadn't believed the story five months ago and he didn't believe it now.

"That's right. Or nearly. Till about eleven, I think."

"Well, what did you do? *Where* did you walk?"

"I can't remember," Evan said. "I went into town for some of the time."

"Did you join up with anyone?"

"I saw a few friends outside the youth club."

"Did you stay with them for any length of time?" Vicky inquired.

"A few minutes, that's all."

Tatton had been trained to remain detached. He neither liked nor loathed suspects in case his feelings clouded his judgement. He regarded the people that he interviewed simply as tools of his trade, not as fellow creatures. He was a trespasser on the privacy of reserved characters like Evan. He didn't enjoy it, but gate-crashing other people's hearts and minds was all part of the job and he didn't easily tolerate those who made his job harder. Clearly, Evan had no alibi for that night. Even if his friends confirmed that they had seen him for a few minutes on Friday night, he could not be eliminated as a suspect. He could have killed his mother, dumped the body, and gone into town specifically to be seen. Tatton did not even bother to ask for the names of the friends Evan claimed to have met that night.

"Let's go back to this argument with your mum," Tatton said, rather irritably. "What did you say it was about?"

"I told you."

Standing behind Evan, Tatton put his hands on the back of the seat in which the boy sat slouched, leaned over him and whispered menacingly, "Tell me again."

Evan chewed at his fingernails as he tried to steel himself. Or maybe he was trying to contain his frustration: an angel trying not to turn into a devil. Still he said nothing.

"Who started it?" Tatton prompted.

"She did," Evan mumbled.

"What did she say?" asked Sergeant McCormick.

"She told me it wasn't my fault."

"What wasn't?"

"That she had a boyfriend."

"She thought you might be blaming yourself, then," Neil Tatton said.

Evan nodded. "I suppose so."

"How did you know she was having an affair?" asked Vicky.

"Because I saw them once. Out on the paper round."

"How do you know they were having a love affair?"

"They were kissing."

"I've kissed lots of women without being . . . romantically attached," DCI Tatton commented.

"Not like they were kissing."

"Okay," the policeman said. "Tell me what he looked like."

"I didn't see his face properly. Quite a bit taller than Mum. Black hair." He shrugged.

"Black hair? Not mousy?"

"Well, it was dark, at any rate."

"Was it long, curly, or what? Was he white, thin, big nose, young, old?"

"It was a long time ago and I only saw him for a second," Evan replied. "He was white, about the same age as Mum, I suppose. He wasn't fat or thin. Average, really. Looked quite smart."

"Did you know him?" Vicky asked. "Had you seen him before?"

"No," Evan answered.

"Let's go back to the argument," Neil said, standing in front of Evan. "*Did* you blame yourself for your mum's behaviour?"

"Why should I?"

"Did you?" Tatton insisted.

"Not really."

"So, how did the conversation go from there?"

Evan shrugged again. "*I* blamed *her*, I suppose.

Said she couldn't think much of us."

"And?"

"And nothing. That was it."

"That was it?"

"We both got a bit annoyed, but that was it."

"Okay," DCI Tatton responded wearily. "What happened then?"

"She went to work. I went to school."

"You didn't see her again?"

Evan shook his head.

"When you came back to the house that night – after this walk – who was in?"

"Just Dad."

"What was he doing?"

"Snoozing in front of the telly," Evan answered.

"No sign of Sarah or Kelly?"

"No."

"All right, Evan, you can go," Tatton said. "But think about something before we see you again: you have a duty to cooperate with us. There's a law about obstructing police officers in the execution of their duties, you know. Think about it."

Evan did not reply. Relieved, he got to his feet and left the dining room as quickly as he could.

DCI Tatton slumped into a chair.

"Doesn't waste his breath, does he?" he grumbled. "Tight as a clam. There's still something he's not letting on about that argument and his walkabout."

"Yes," Vicky agreed. "But it could be purely innocent, or just irrelevant. I'm sure that fifteen-year-olds get up to plenty that they wouldn't want to tell the police. It doesn't have to be murder."

"Mmm." Detective Chief Inspector Tatton sighed, then said, "Go and drag in the daughters. Not that it'll do us much good. Another dose of *déjà vu* for me. Kelly first."

He was right. They learned nothing new from Kelly and Sarah. Any one of a number of friends could confirm that Kelly had been dancing herself silly that night. She only chilled out in the early hours. Sarah's boyfriend, Matt Smith, could confirm that they'd watched a film in town that night. She'd returned at eleven thirty. Neither daughter had seen anything but both had guessed that their mother had a boyfriend. In their separate ways, each revealed her feelings about her mother's death. Kelly remained stiffly solemn as if scared to betray her emotions in front of strangers, while Sarah fidgeted and trembled on the verge of weeping. After the interviews Neil Tatton left the Keatings' house with nothing extra to show.

The manager of The Seafood Spree, Daniel Perriman, was a different kettle of fish. Years of making clients feel welcome and comfortable had fashioned his face. Like an airline steward, he wore a permanent professional smile and exuded friendliness. Behind closed doors, though, he probably ranted and raved at his staff if he found a speck of dirt on the cutlery. Vicky imagined a taskmaster who was nervous and demanding in private, and an unflappable host in public.

He escorted the police to a discreet table and, out of habit, took hold of the back of the chair as if he were about to invite Vicky to sit. "As I recall, this was the lady's place," he said. "The gentleman sat opposite. So, you see, my staff and I could see her clearly but the gentleman had his back to us. He leaned across the table and took her hand now and again."

"Did they come together or did they meet in here?" Tatton inquired.

"They came in together, I think. Most do."

"And they left . . . when?" asked Vicky.

The restaurant manager shrugged and answered politely, "It was over five months ago, you know."

"You said they came in at about six and left at seven thirty originally. Your first customers," Neil reminded him.

"Then I'm sure I was right," Mr Perriman replied. "I remember it was definitely early."

"And you said the man had mousy hair."

"Did I? You have to understand that I've had

thousands of customers since then. I really don't know for sure."

Neil persisted. "Your statement referred to mousy coloured hair. Not, say, black."

"Well, I hope I got it right. I could describe the lady much more accurately."

DCI Tatton smiled wryly. "I don't need a description of her, only him."

Mr Perriman's expression conveyed helplessness. "I'm sorry."

The manager was ten times more talkative and cooperative than Evan but he knew ten times less, the detective thought. As a result both of them were equally unhelpful as witnesses. Neil Tatton hadn't expected anything else. He was relying on Henderson's Builders and the forensic report to supply him with new leads.

4

Evan shuffled impatiently from foot to foot as he waited for someone at the other end of the line to pick up the phone. In agitation, he drummed on the window of the call box with the ragged fingers of his right hand. "Come on!" he muttered into the receiver.

Eventually, the ringing stopped and a male voice said bluntly, "Yes?"

Evan recognized the brief response. "Mr Warr," he breathed. "Evan Keating here."

"Oh." The man seemed to anticipate trouble.

"Have you heard?"

"Of course I heard," Trevor Warr replied. "No one drives across your garden and knocks a whacking great hole in my factory wall without me knowing about it. I've been to see the damage."

"But that wasn't all."

"Yes. I heard," he said. "I'm sorry. Sorry about your mother."

"But what are you going to do now?"

Warr didn't answer immediately. The question took him by surprise. "Get the factory fixed and back in action as quickly as possible. What else?"

"What about Mum? Have the police been to see you?"

"What do you mean, Evan? I can do nothing about your mother. That little problem has nothing to do with me. And yes, a constable came to see me, as you'd expect, but only to tell me about the wall."

"What about the planning permission row and . . . you know?"

"I imagine your mum made herself unpopular with a whole number of people, not just me." Warr's tone suggested annoyance as he added, "I repeat, I had nothing to do with her death."

This time, Evan hesitated. He simply did not believe Warr. But he hoped that the owner of the video factory could convince the police of his innocence if they ever got close to him. He dreaded the possible arrest and conviction of Warr. He needed him. "Okay," he said into the mouthpiece. "Good. But I . . . er . . . need some weekend work. Any going at the moment?"

Warr laughed. "You've got to be joking! Not

unless you're a budding builder. I've had to close down the operation till the wall's replaced. Even then, with your mother and all . . . it's a bit of a risk for me."

Evan crammed both the receiver and his fingernails up to his mouth. "Look, I'd come in, wouldn't ask any questions, and do whatever you want me to do. I won't be any trouble and I need the cash. Please!" he pleaded.

"Calm down, Evan. When the building's fixed and the fuss has died down a bit, we'll be back up and running. I'll think about it then. But get this straight: I'm not promising. There are plenty of people out there who'd take on a bit of extra work for something straight into their pockets. We all need it these days."

"Yes, but . . ." Evan ran out of reasoning and resorted to threats. "The cops are coming back to talk to me again. You wouldn't want them to learn about your . . . arguments with Mum, would you?"

Warr snorted. "They'll unearth our disagreements over planning permission sooner or later."

"But it wasn't just that, was it? She found out about my work for you. She didn't . . . approve."

Warr became defensive. "She didn't see me about that, so don't try and make out that she did."

"But the police—" Evan began.

"You won't get my sympathy with threats,"

Warr interrupted him. "You won't tell the police any more than you have to, not if you value the money you get from me. You need it too much to let on to the law."

Evan knew that it was true. He could not reveal his suspicions about Trevor Warr to the police without telling them everything. Then where would he be? In trouble himself.

"I'll be in touch," Warr whispered into his ear, "when I have some news – when we're back in operation."

Evan thumped the tattered telephone directory. "All right," he muttered, admitting the weakness of his position. He put down the phone and went home, where the scaffolding in the garden prevented him from taking out his frustration on the wall with a football.

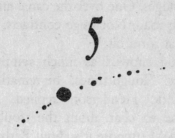

5

The police officers pulled into Henderson's yard and parked between a concrete mixer and a dump truck. Amid the chaos of his office, Eric Henderson was both wary of the police and yet still slick.

"How's the construction industry?" Tatton asked him. "As bad as they say?"

"Probably worse. I've laid off quite a few workers, I'm afraid. Every contract is priceless these days – and fought for. You have to run a lean operation to stay in business."

"You didn't make Mrs Keating redundant, did you?" Vicky asked, well aware that she was addressing her own husband's employer.

"No. But look at this office. I needed someone

like her full-time to keep it in order. She only worked part-time here. And her replacement does just two days a week."

"Any good jobs on at the moment – or in the offing?"

"A few bridges. One over the canal and three for the new ring road. Not huge contracts, but they'll keep us afloat for a bit."

DCI Tatton showed as much sympathy as he could muster. "Tough times," he remarked.

"True," Eric Henderson replied. "But you haven't come to chat about the troubles of the building trade. I suppose it's about Barbara Keating and, from what I read in the papers, a rather gruesome find."

Neil Tatton nodded. "And in your wall too."

"Yes. That was one of our contracts. Clinched it in September, and started shortly after. It was for a Mr Warr, a video manufacturer, extending his business premises, in a hurry." The builder shook his head and added, "Ironic really, getting that contract."

"Why do you say that?"

"Well, Barbara Keating fought for ages over the planning permission. She didn't want it erected. Then, by working here, she found herself helping to build it – in an indirect way, of course."

"Did she ever talk to you about the extension?" asked Vicky.

Henderson thought for a moment then replied, "Not as I recall."

"If I were her," Neil Tatton suggested, "I might have tried to persuade you not to build it. I might have thought about sabotage."

"Sabotage?" Henderson queried. "You mean, she was up to something that night? Fell into the cavity and knocked herself out? Next day my lads tipped concrete mix . . ." He did not continue.

"It crossed my mind," the policeman said.

"Possibly," Henderson replied. "It's a horrible thought but I can't comment one way or the other. All I know is, she didn't approach me about the building site. She knew I needed the work and if I'd broken the contract we'd all have been out of a job and someone else would have built it anyway. If she wanted to halt the building, she'd have had to nobble Warr, not me. There was a queue of builders wanting the work. There always is these days. Only Warr could have stopped it. Perhaps you'd better talk to him."

"We will." DCI Tatton tried a different line of questioning. "How well did you know Barbara Keating?"

"She was a work colleague. I wouldn't say I was close to her."

"Did you ever meet socially?"

"No."

"How do you think she got on with her family?"

Eric Henderson frowned at the police officers. "She didn't bring her problems with her to work – if she had any," he added smartly, "so I've no idea."

"For a moment there, it seemed you were suggesting that she *did* have problems at home."

"Well," Eric said, realizing that it was futile to deny the policeman's allegation, "there were rumours about an affair."

Eagerly, Tatton asked, "An affair with who?"

"I've no idea. I don't even know if it was true. And I wasn't bothered to find out. She could have been married to ten separate men for all I cared. Her personal life was her own business, not mine."

"Did you ever see her with another man?" Sergeant McCormick queried in her low-pitched tone.

"Sure," he replied, barely disguising his contempt for the question. "I saw her with your husband." He paused for effect, looking directly at Vicky, then added, "And with Ted, the warehouse manager, and Graham from Personnel. She'd even been seen with me. Need I go on?"

"I meant," she said, "obviously romantically involved."

"When she was here, she was involved with letters, phone calls, orders, dealing with visitors. That sort of thing. Any romance she enjoyed was out of hours. So I wouldn't know about it."

"Thank you," Vicky responded.

Before they left Henderson's, the two police officers talked to three of the men who had worked on the video factory the previous October. They remembered the night of Friday the thirteenth. They'd joked about it. They were behind schedule, and working late under floodlights. They'd just started pouring in the concrete when the generator failed – typical for Friday the thirteenth. They couldn't remember exactly when they gave up and left the site – probably about eight thirty. They finished the concreting at first light on the next morning. And, no, they hadn't looked into the cavity before they filled in the remainder with concrete.

On the way back to the police station, Neil Tatton thought aloud for his colleague's benefit. "What have we got, then? A rotten Friday for Barbara Keating, I suppose. But a picture is emerging. First, a breakfast row with her son. A day at work. Then, at about six o'clock, she met her lover, Mr Fish, and together they went for a meal. And a scheming discussion. They left the restaurant together at seven thirty. An hour later, the labourers had left Warr's new factory. That gives ample time for a murder and travel to the building site. Her body could have been dumped there in the dark any time after eight thirty and before dawn on Saturday."

"But only by someone who knew about the site," Vicky put in.

"So which of our suspects does that rule out?"

"None of them," Vicky admitted. "But it implies that Mr Fish *did* know about it, if he's our man."

"True," Neil replied. "But he might not be. She could have left him and gone home. There was still plenty of time for her husband to do her in and dump the body before the kids came back. His alibi's hardly worthy of the name."

"The daughters seem to be in the clear, though. Their alibis held up."

"Mmm. Unlike Evan's. And," Tatton continued, "he's big. Powerful enough to drag a body up a few ramps on the building site."

"But the boy seems the most cut up about her death," Vicky noted. "It's got the girls down all right and Keating himself is angry, but Evan could be in real shock."

"I doubt it," Tatton argued. "He's just unco-operative. And remember, they've all had months to get used to the idea of being motherless. I wouldn't expect them to be devastated."

"What about Warr?" Vicky tried. "There's a new suspect. He'd probably keep an eye on progress at the building site, so he'd know there was scope for dumping a corpse there."

"Motive?" Neil inquired.

"If planning permission was such a nightmare,

perhaps he came to blows with Barbara Keating over it. It would've been very convenient for Warr to get rid of her."

"But she copped it *after* she'd lost the battle over planning permission."

"Ah, yes. Perhaps she was taking her revenge on him, then, but he turned the tables on her."

"You mean, she attacked him in some way, and he killed her in the struggle? Then he hid the body because he was scared."

"Who knows?" Vicky replied.

"Mmm," Tatton murmured thoughtfully. "Remember there wasn't an obvious weapon. No knife wounds or bullet holes. So she didn't have her own weapon turned against her. That suggests she attacked him with bare hands. Let's go and take a look at him. If he's some muscle-bound hunk, I think we can forget it. She wouldn't risk it."

Trevor Warr was fifty, balding, and a bit of a wimp. His house made up for it, though. It was enormous, full of strong colours and beautiful objects. Neil looked round the lounge. "Nice house," he whispered to his colleague. "Business must be booming."

After the detective had explained to Warr why they wanted to question him, Tatton said, "The British public must be snapping up videos if you think a bigger factory is viable."

Warr was dressed casually but expensively, with an outlandish medallion around his neck. "Yes," he answered with self-satisfaction. "There are worse businesses to be in."

"What exactly do you make in your factory?"

"We manufacture videos, thousands of copies from a master tape. Under licence, you understand. Then we distribute them. When you browse around in your video shop, there's a good chance you'll pick up one that my company's produced."

"You don't do the actual filming, then? Just distributing other people's films."

"That's right. It's like publishing. Taking a story someone else has written and churning out the books. In my case, the story's on tape."

"Interesting," DCI Tatton commented in a tone that suggested the opposite. "Your new place, it's been in operation for a few months now. Did you go on to the site when it was being built?"

"Not much."

"But you did?"

"Yes. I must admit to being a workaholic," the small man replied. "I went in now and again to see how the building was getting on. Couldn't wait to get going, you see. The builders were behind schedule and I went to chivvy them along."

Vicky imagined that a man like Mr Warr was more likely to antagonize the workers than speed them up, but she kept the thought to herself and asked, "So were you there in the early part of October?"

"Probably, I can't be sure, though."

"Did you get planning permission easily?" Tatton queried.

"No," Warr sneered. "A local woman kept trying to block it, but I got there eventually."

"And do you know what happened to that local woman?"

"Yes," he answered. "I read about it in the newspapers. I'm sorry, but I can't say I'm heart-broken. She seemed to me to be a most obstructive and unpleasant individual."

"Did you ever meet her? Face to face?"

"Only across various council rooms during our little tussle. That was close enough."

"Where were you on the night of Friday the thirteenth of October?"

"You don't think I . . ." Warr paused, then added, "Of course, you're just doing your job and I can see why I might be regarded as a suspect. Just a moment." He took a diary from a bureau and immediately put it down again, mumbling, "Last year's, not this." He searched for a while then, from the bottom of a pile, drew out another desk planner. "October thirteen," he muttered as he flicked through the pages. "During the day," he announced, "I had a meeting in London at the BBC. Plans afoot to release a certain

45

series on video. I can't say which. Hush hush."

"But you can tell us who you met."

"Yes. A Mr Harding in Publicity."

"What time did you get back?"

"Late. I stopped in London to do some research round the cinemas."

"Research?"

"Watched a couple of new films. But neither was suitable for video, by my estimation." For the police officers' benefit, he recited details of the films and the cinemas that he had visited.

"And you got home when?" Vicky queried.

Warr breathed in deeply then exhaled while he considered. "I don't really know. Not far short of midnight, I shouldn't wonder."

"You made this trip alone?" Neil inquired.

"Yes."

"Can I see your diary?"

"Of course."

The scribbling in the box for 13th October appeared to confirm Warr's trip to the BBC but there was no record of watching films. DCI Tatton queried this.

"No. I was in London and unexpectedly I had the time after my meeting. The films that I wanted to view were on, so I went. Spur of the moment decision. No plans, so it didn't get into my planner."

"I see," Tatton said, rising from his chair and calling a halt to the interview.

"Have you got all you need from me?" Warr checked.

"For the moment," Tatton replied, with a hint of malice in his voice.

As Vicky accelerated out of Warr's drive and rain began to splash on to the windscreen, Neil turned to her. "Another one without a good alibi for Friday night," he commented. "But I'm still not convinced about his motive. I'm going to pay the forensic team a visit. We need a lead – or a lucky break. Perhaps they can provide one. You check out the London films."

The Chief Forensic Scientist was dragged out of the laboratories to speak to Neil Tatton. She had a manic mass of pure white hair reaching down to her white lab coat, and an obvious passion for her work. "Keating?" she chirped. "Yes. Messy, eh?"

"But what have you found, Kate?"

"Come this way," she said brightly, indicating the way to her disorderly office. "I'll show you my new toy – a LIMS."

"A what?"

Kate beamed. She was enjoying her ability to bamboozle Neil, and was just waiting for an opportunity to show off her new gadget. She waved her arms vigorously in the air as she spelled it out, "It's a laboratory information management system."

"You mean, it's a computer."

"Yes. Here it is."

As they sat in front of the screen, Neil said, "What happened to the good old days when someone just told me the findings? You know, when we used to *talk* to each other."

"Much more sophisticated now. The tests are specialized. Lots of different expertise needed, so you'd have to speak to the Toxicology Lab, the analytical chemists, microscopists. It's endless. But this," she said, patting her electronic box of tricks as if it were an obedient dog, "knows it all. Every result from every lab is recorded in a file in here. Immediate access. No messing," she enthused.

She tapped out a password and the screen came to life with a plan of the Keatings' garden and details of Barbara Keating's death. "Microscopy's reporting fibres found on the body and clothing. Some from the seats in The Seafood Spree restaurant, and some grey-blue fibres possibly from a Peugeot car seat. But," she warned, "there may be other sources. There were also some green woollen fibres, probably from a jumper. Pathology seems to be bemused. No detectable physical injury and no sign of a struggle. The cause of death isn't obvious."

"What about poisoning?" Tatton asked.

Kate clicked the mouse on the toxicology icon. "Here we are. Everything at your fingertips. Good stuff, eh? Anyway," she noted from the screen, "nothing of significance found but any poison is likely to have degraded over a few months, so the lab wouldn't be able to detect it."

"Great," Neil uttered sarcastically.

"I doubt if you're interested in the contents of the gut, barely recognizable after this time, but analysis suggested muesli for breakfast – wheat grain and oats still in the stomach. There was some evidence of a shrimp salad as well."

"That figures," Neil muttered. "Anything else?"

"Bound to be," Kate replied. "Let's try chemical analysis." She clicked on two more icons and another report appeared. "No. Nothing unusual in the body or in the handbag. But that reminds me – there was something in her bag that'll interest you," she commented tantalizingly.

Neil's ears pricked up. "Really? What?"

"Just a second." She accessed yet another computerized report – a list of the contents of Mrs Keating's handbag. Among the traditional items – make-up, purse, tissues – there was one that had been highlighted. A piece of paper, 6 cm by 3 cm, printed with "Dinner Date. 10. 6."

Kate looked into Neil's face and muttered, "I was right, wasn't I? You're intrigued."

"Mmm." He was fascinated but, if he had

deduced anything of importance, he kept it to himself. "Anything else of interest?"

"Not really," Kate replied. Then she added, "Well, there was a used envelope, addressed to Henderson's Builders. Nothing in it."

"I'll take it – and that bit of paper."

It took the forensic scientist a couple of minutes to find the items and hand them over – an ordinary envelope and the scrap of paper, both sealed inside plastic bags. Neil thanked her and hurried away to find Sergeant McCormick. They needed to pay the Keating family another visit.

Kelly looked at Sarah and Sarah looked at Kelly. Then they both looked at the blank faces of their father and brother. On the small piece of paper that DCI Tatton showed them, "Dinner Date" had been typed at the top. Underneath, it was inscribed with the figure ten and, under that, six. "No," Mr Keating muttered. "No idea what that's about."

Tatton turned to the youngsters. "What about you three?" he said. "Any ideas?" Kelly shrugged and the other two mumbled, "No."

"Okay," DCI Tatton replied. "Have any of you got green woollen jumpers? Or did you have one five or six months ago?"

"Yes," Kelly answered. "Why?"

"Because it might explain some fibres we found on your mum's body. With your permission, we'll take a few fibres from your jumper before we leave, so we can test for a match with the ones we found."

"All right," Kelly murmured.

"What make of car have you got?"

"A Cavalier," Mr Keating answered.

"What type of seats, or seat covers, does it have? What colour?"

"Some sort of plastic – dark colour."

"And did you have it in October?" asked Vicky.

"Yes," Mr Keating replied testily.

"How about this?" The detective showed Clive Keating a tatty envelope, with Henderson's business address typed on it.

Clive smiled wryly. "Over there," he said, pointing to the sideboard behind Sarah, "there's still a drawer stuffed full of them." Sarah leaned back in her chair, yanked a bulging polythene bag of used stamps torn from envelopes from the drawer, and dangled it in the air. "Barbara collected them for charity," her father explained. "When I remember, I keep them as well."

"Mmm." Chief Inspector Tatton stood up. "For breakfast, was your wife in the habit of eating muesli?" he asked.

Clive's face betrayed amazement and anger at the same time. "What's that got to do with it?"

"Probably nothing," he replied. "But I'm curious. Just making sure that it checks out with what we've found."

"The answer's yes," Clive snapped. "She did."

"Thanks," Tatton said. Turning to Kelly he added, "Can you fetch us that jumper? And a bit of sticky tape."

"Tape?"

"We'll just press it against the material for a moment to take a sample of the fibres."

"Oh, I see," Kelly said. "Okay." She went upstairs to get the jumper while Sarah fetched a roll of Sellotape and scissors.

Two days later, shortly after Kate reported that Kelly's jumper did not match the fibres found on her mother's body, the meagre pieces of evidence became irrelevant to the investigation. With a heart-felt sigh of relief, Tatton wrapped it all up. He was able to go to the Keatings early on Friday morning with the good news that the murderer had confessed. The case was closed.

Sergeant McCormick was on compassionate leave, so he turned up at the Keatings' house with a different side-kick.

"Oh," Kelly said as she answered the door. "It's you."

"May I come in? I have some news that you'll find . . . interesting."

The sparkle in the detective's eye told her that he'd solved the crime. She stood to one side. "Okay," she replied. "We're having breakfast, but you'd better come in."

Looking like the cat that got the cream, DCI Tatton stood in front of the family in the dining room and announced, "Late last night, we found Mrs Keating's killer, a man we called Mr Fish and whose real name I'll come to in a minute." He looked at his stunned audience as if he expected applause.

Kelly was the first to find her voice. "You arrested him?" she asked.

"Not exactly," Tatton replied. "There was no need." Too impatient even to sit, he looked down on them like an actor in full flow. "Let me tell you the events of Friday the thirteenth last year." Looking directly at Clive Keating for a moment, he added, "It might even give you some comfort." He cleared his throat and declared, "I believe things came to a head for Barbara Keating that day. She was under pressure from her boyfriend, Mr Fish, to leave all of you and go away with him." The detective returned Clive's stare, saying, "Yes, there *was* a lover, as you will hear in a moment. But first, there was Evan." Evan stopped chewing his fingernails and cocked his head. "You and your mum had your . . . discussion. Being accused of unfaithfulness and not caring about the family only added to her feeling that she had to make a decision. In fact, Evan's comments probably tipped the balance. At work she got a note from Mr Fish, saying they should meet for a dinner date. Remember, I showed you the slip of paper."

Kelly interrupted, asking, "What about the ten and six? What did they have to do with it?"

"I don't think it's a coincidence that The Seafood Spree is 10 Tanglefoot Road and that they met there after work at six o'clock. Anyway," he continued, "Mr Fish gave her an ultimatum – it's either them or me." Neil paused for effect. "She decided then and there. Her argument with you, Evan, made her realize how much she'd hurt you. Hurt you all, I imagine. She called off the affair."

Clive blurted out, "How do you know all this? You're just guessing. It could be nonsense."

"I don't think so. We have Mr Fish's word for most of it," DCI Tatton replied. "That night, Mr Fish was so upset by her decision that he killed her. He couldn't bear to lose her, so he decided you wouldn't have her either. It was after the meal, dark. They left at seven thirty. He drove over here in his Peugeot and dumped the body, sometime after eight thirty, in the cavity where the concrete was about to be poured. He knew all about the building site, you see." He warded off their questions by raising both hands. "I'm coming to who he is in a minute. He resumed his normal life – and his work at Henderson's Builders where he'd met Mrs Keating – but couldn't forget what he'd done. We know from his own wife that he'd been miserable since October, and acting oddly, so it all fits." He coughed, then continued. "The discovery of her body brought it all back to him. Guilt." He shook his head. "He couldn't live with what he'd done. For five months or so he'd tried, but failed. Last night, at nine o'clock, he committed suicide." The detective took a photograph out of his pocket and showed it to Evan. "Is this the man you saw with your mum?" he asked.

Evan took a look and hardly hesitated. He nodded. "That's him."

"You're sure? There's no doubt at all in your mind that it's the man you saw kissing your mum?"

"No. It's him."

"I have to tell you," the detective said, putting the photograph back into his pocket, "that Mr Fish was Detective Sergeant Vicky McCormick's husband. He didn't match the restaurant owner's first description particularly well, but when I showed him McCormick's face, it jogged his memory. Like Evan, he identified McCormick as Mr Fish."

The detective's performance was nearly at an end. For an encore, he read from McCormick's suicide note. "'She promised she would leave her husband. But she changed her mind. She did not want to see me again. I did not mean to kill her.' We found this – and more besides – on his computer screen. It seems that the word processor's taken over from writing in all walks of life, even suicide notes. Anyway, it's a clear confession. Everything fits. I'm closing the case." He looked pleased, pleased to wash his hands of the whole business and get on to another case. It was a swift and tidy ending.

Again, Kelly looked at Sarah and Sarah looked at Kelly. This time, it was not surprise but disbelief that they exchanged through their expressions. Their dad and Evan simply looked relieved.

"So," Kelly piped up, "Mr McCormick had a green jumper?"

"The fibres weren't from your jumper, but the forensic service is overworked," the policeman replied. "Now there's a clear-cut outcome, I won't be wasting their time on unnecessary work. All in all, it's best to let sleeping dogs lie. A sad and sorry affair, but at least it's over."

As soon as they closed the door on the policeman, the sisters shot upstairs to Kelly's room. Carefully closing the bedroom door, Sarah ventured, "What do you think?"

Kelly shook her head wearily. "We lost Mum ages ago. She wasn't coming back. She loved some-one else. I don't believe it."

"Nor me," Sarah said. "I can't see her wanting to try again with Dad."

Kelly plonked herself down in a chair. "There is a problem, though. If not, lots of problems."

"Oh?"

"If we don't believe she was going to start again with Dad, we don't believe the suicide note. If we don't believe the note, we don't believe it was suicide."

"You mean, Mr McCormick was murdered as well?"

Stuffing her papers into her school bag, Kelly nodded. "The suicide note was typed, he said, not hand-written. So there was no writing to check against Mr McCormick's. Anyone could have typed it into his computer."

"I suppose so," Sarah murmured.

"But there's something else."

"What?"

Kelly looked puzzled. "If McCormick was her boyfriend, why didn't he report her missing? All the time, the story in the papers was that Mum had run off with someone. Obviously he knew that was wrong, so why didn't he say so? Perhaps we're wrong about all this."

Sarah thought about it then replied excitedly, "No, we're right. He wouldn't go to the police because of his wife. She's a policewoman. He didn't want his wife to know about the affair."

"Yes. Could well be," Kelly agreed. "But if McCormick didn't kill Mum, who did?"

"And," Sarah added, "who killed Mr McCormick and faked the suicide note?"

The girls looked at each other helplessly.

"I think we'd better try and find out," Kelly said, as they made for the front door.

6

Physically the two sisters were quite unalike. Kelly was tall and thin, with fair hair cut short, scraggy and boyish to offset the natural delicacy of her pale face. She had never felt delicate but she had been cursed with those features. Sarah was shorter but, like their mother, more robust. Her hair was longer and darker. Despite appearances, she was more sensitive than her older sister.

In Kelly's room after school, Sarah was sprawled on the bed. "It's all very well playing cops and robbers – cops and murderer, actually – but it just doesn't seem right, this . . . picking over Mum's bones." She sighed heavily. "Poor old Mum."

Kelly touched her arm lightly. "I know, but it beats moping about. It's something we *can* do for her: find out what really happened. We can't do much else."

"I suppose not," Sarah mumbled her agreement. She sniffed and said, "All right. But what do we do? Where do we start?"

Kelly shrugged. "I'm not exactly an expert at this sort of thing either. My only qualification is watching cops on the box. And who knows how realistic they are?" She hesitated then suggested, "We could make a list, though. You know – suspects and clues. Stuff like that."

Sarah disentangled the fingers of her right hand from her hair and smiled sadly. "Okay. Sounds sensible, I suppose." She scrambled off the bed and over to Kelly's desk.

Clearing a space among the bottles and jars, Kelly put a piece of paper in front of them. Her Biro hovered over it.

"Well?" Sarah murmured.

"Suspects," Kelly said. "I was just thinking."

"I suppose," Sarah muttered gloomily, "you're going to tell me that if we're going to do this properly we've got to start with Dad and Evan."

Kelly nodded. "I suppose so."

"What about you and me?" Sarah asked.

Kelly grimaced. "I think we can leave ourselves off. Besides, we've both got alibis for the night Mum died."

"True," Sarah responded rapidly.

"That reminds me," Kelly added. "What about last night? If McCormick was killed last night at nine o'clock," she said in a whisper, "have Dad and Evan got alibis? That would mean we don't have to put them down."

"Dad was working. Late night Thursday opening, then he'd be off doing the rounds collecting newspaper money from his old dears. That takes till about nine. The trouble is," she added, "we can't be sure that he went on the rounds last night. Sometimes he does it every other Thursday. And Evan – he was doing whatever Evan does, no doubt. Hanging about."

Kelly had no reason to hesitate further. She headed the list with her father and Evan. Against each person on their hit list, the sisters added a possible motive. Against their father there were just two words: unfaithfulness, jealousy. Evan's motive was put down as an unknown argument. Looking for other suspects, Sarah asked, "Who was the man Mum clashed with over the video factory?"

"Warr," answered Kelly. "I'll put him down under planning permission argument."

They also included Eric Henderson. They didn't know of any reason why he would want to murder their mum but noted that he would be no stranger to the building site and so had the knowledge to dispose of her body.

"Then there's Vicky McCormick," Kelly added.

"That's if she knew about the building work as well."

"But she's a policewoman," Sarah objected.

"So what? I don't suppose the police are immune to crimes of passion."

"She killed Mum because she was . . . stealing her husband. Okay," Sarah agreed, "but why would she kill her own husband?"

Kelly pondered for a moment. "I know. McCormick – Mr McCormick, that is – didn't go to the police even when it was reported that Mum had run off with someone. Right? He couldn't. But he'd be curious, surely. Maybe he did some investigating himself instead. The detective said he'd been behaving strangely for a good part of the last six months."

"Yes," Sarah interrupted in her eagerness. "If he got close to the real murderer, then he might have got himself killed."

"Exactly," Kelly joined in. "His wife might have killed him and faked his suicide if he was about to turn her in."

"True. But it could have been anyone. If he found out who killed Mum, then the killer would have to get rid of him as well. It could have been his wife – or anyone on the list."

"Or someone who's not on the list," Kelly interjected. "We might not have thought of him yet."

"Or her," Sarah added.

They left a few blank lines on the page in case they needed to add more names later, then wrote down some clues that they would need to follow up: a green jumper; Evan's argument; the Dinner Date note; the seafood restaurant owner's description that didn't quite fit; knowledge of the building site; McCormick's murder at 9 pm on Thursday; the 5½ month gap between murders; a Peugeot car.

"A Peugeot?" Sarah queried.

"Don't you remember? A couple of days ago, Tatton was into car seats in a big way when he questioned us. This morning he said McCormick drove a Peugeot. Not just a car but a Peugeot. They must have found something from Peugeot seats on Mum."

"Yes, you're right," Sarah said. "But there are plenty of Peugeots in this world. And even if Mr McCormick didn't do it, she might still have been in his car before . . . you know. Perfectly innocent."

"I know. But there are even more green jumpers in this world and that's on our list. By the way, Evan's got a green pullover, though he didn't admit it to the police. Still, let's not worry about that just now. On its own, each of these things I'm writing down isn't very helpful, but we're chasing someone with the right combination. Yes? We're building up a picture."

"You mean, someone in an environmentally

friendly jumper who can change his appearance and drives around in a Peugeot?"

Kelly grinned. "Okay, I take your point, but you know what I mean."

"So do we now borrow Dad's car and cruise the back streets for this chameleon?"

"I don't think so, somehow. Let's keep it in the family."

Feeling glum about the prospect, Sarah asked, "You want to start with our very own black sheep?"

"Can't think of anything better," Kelly admitted.

Deprived of the concrete wall, Evan was juggling the football and counting at each kick, "Ten. Eleven. Twelve."

"Tricky," Kelly said, buttering him up. "I don't know how you do that."

Evan didn't lose his concentration easily but, unaccustomed to praise, he faltered. The ball hit the ground at fourteen. Even so, he didn't appear to be upset that they had spoiled his record attempt. In fact, he was always so docile that they had never seen him annoyed. That was one reason why neither sister really believed he was guilty of murder. If he ever did get angry, then he did it in private or at least out of sight of Kelly and Sarah. Now he squinted suspiciously at his sisters and prompted, "Yes?"

"You're really skilful with a ball, Evan," Sarah said. "Why don't you join a team? I bet Matt would get you a place in the Scorpions."

"I prefer it on my own," Evan returned.

"You know this investigation?" asked Kelly.

"The one that's over?"

"Sort of."

"What do you mean?"

"We," Sarah said, nodding towards Kelly, "don't think the police got it right."

Evan sighed. "It's over. Let it go."

"Do *you* think Tatton got it right?" Kelly insisted.

Evan bounced the football twice, then replied, "That's got nothing to do with it. I'm just glad the law won't be snooping around any more."

"So," Sarah deduced, "you think there's more to it as well. McCormick isn't the whole answer."

"So?" Evan mumbled, increasingly disgruntled with his sisters' attitude.

"So we ought to try to find out what really happened," Kelly replied.

"Why?"

"Because . . . because we want to know the truth. There's a murderer out there somewhere. Who knows who else is on his hit list?"

Reinforcing the point, Sarah added, "Maybe we are."

"Don't be daft," Evan said disdainfully. "What

are you anyway? A couple of Miss Marples?"

Kelly shrugged. "Something like that." And before Evan could pour more scorn on them, she said, "You know this row you had with Mum?"

For an instant, Evan looked amazed and disgusted. "You don't think I . . ." His voice faded away and immediately he began to juggle the ball again. "One. Two. Three." It was his way of avoiding the issue.

Now Sarah decided to have a go. "You're not the sort to have a real row," she said.

"Well," Evan replied, still keeping the ball off the ground, "perhaps it wasn't a real row, more an exchange of views."

"But what was it about – really? Not what you told the police."

In frustration, Evan kicked the ball out of reach. "It was exactly like I told them."

"Was there something else, then? Something you didn't tell?"

"That's my business. And Mum's."

Kelly and Sarah stole a glance at each other.

"Come on," Kelly persisted. "You can tell us. It might be the key to this whole thing."

Evan strolled across the lawn to pick up the football. When he returned with it, he walked straight past his sisters, mumbling, "No. I don't think so."

"Do you know who killed Mum?" Sarah called after him.

When Evan looked back without stopping and muttered, "No idea," neither Kelly nor Sarah believed him.

In desperation, Kelly shouted, "Mum would want you to tell us. She'd want us to get to the bottom of it. See it from her point of view."

Evan hesitated, turned, and said, "She doesn't have one any more." He slouched back into the house.

The two sisters shrugged at each other. "Oh, well," Kelly murmured, "could be worse."

"I suppose so," Sarah replied. She exhaled loudly as if she were tired. "What about Dad? Should we check him out somehow?"

Kelly thought about it. "No green jumpers, no Peugeot. And . . . well . . . it's Dad. I'd have trouble believing that he could . . ."

"Yeah," Sarah agreed. "I know."

"And I don't know what to ask him. 'Did you kill Mum?' seems pretty heartless! As well as pointless. I couldn't do it."

"Let's ignore that angle for the moment, then. He's not a prime suspect."

Kelly smiled. "You've been watching too much telly," she said.

Together they went indoors to discuss their next move.

7

The next move, they decided, was to put pressure on Evan. Neither Kelly nor Sarah were keen on this tactic, but they recognized that he was their best lead. They had little choice. Yet it seemed doubly underhand to investigate Evan: he was their brother and he was vulnerable.

They decided not to follow him on Saturday morning when he got on his bike, delivered the newspapers and then collected his earnings from the shop. Late in the afternoon, though, when he headed for the town centre, they went in hot pursuit. They ended up at Revolvers – a popular Saturday-night spot for kids. The place was throbbing with music and Kelly and Sarah had to shout to make themselves heard. Roller skaters charged up and down, round and round the rink, occasionally skating into the family area, zipping expertly hither and thither among tables and chairs. A cluster of youngsters was gathered round the large TV screen showing a soccer match. If the music hadn't been so deafening, they would have heard the thump and clatter of ten-pin bowlers and the crack of snooker balls upstairs in the club.

Evan did not join the queue for roller skates or bowling shoes. He bought a packet of crisps from the bar, then sat at a table near the television and watched the football, slowly eating crisps and occasionally nibbling at his fingernails. Kelly and Sarah took up a position at the other side of the family area and kept an eye on him from a distance, while skaters criss-crossed their view.

"What's he up to?" Sarah yelled into her sister's ear.

"Well, right now he's scratching his head as if he's got nits."

"Don't muck about! What's he really doing?"

Kelly shrugged. "Strikes me he's watching the soccer on the box," she said with dry humour.

"Yes, but . . ."

"I know," Kelly replied. "He could've watched it at home. Perhaps he likes the atmosphere. Perhaps he's meeting someone. A girl, maybe."

Sarah smiled weakly. Kelly's comment reminded her that she was snooping on her own brother, and she blushed. If he had come to meet a girl, Sarah would feel mean and guilty for prying into his private affairs.

On the big screen, the soccer match ended and the scene switched to a race course. Long-legged horses, only just under control, were being paraded before the race.

Still Evan watched avidly. No one joined him, but at one point a beefy male acquaintance walked past him, nodded a greeting, and paused briefly to take a crisp from the bag that Evan offered him. The man smiled his thanks and walked away. Evan finished the crisps and threw away the empty packet.

A few minutes later, the same man ambled past Evan and thrust his own bag of crisps towards him. From where they stood, Kelly and Sarah could see the words "fair exchange" on the man's lips. Evan's hand dipped eagerly into the packet, but he did not eat the titbit that he took. Instead, he slipped it into his pocket.

As the man with the crisps walked briskly away, Sarah said, "What was all that about?"

"I don't know," Kelly answered, "but not just an exchange of crisps. I've got an idea. Not a nice one. Keep an eye on Evan – I'll be back in a minute." She shot after Evan's friend.

"Careful!" Sarah called after her.

On the television, the horses shuffled into line

under starter's orders.

Three or four minutes later Kelly returned and, sitting close to Sarah, shouted into her ear, "He took a crisp from a girl over there, then got into a Peugeot and sorted something out on his lap. I couldn't see what. Now he's come back in."

The sound of the music was mixed with the thunderous pounding of hooves.

When the race was over, Evan seemed to lose interest. He nodded glumly towards his acquaintance and sauntered towards the exit.

Kelly nudged her sister. "Come on," she said. "We might as well tackle him. Now's as good a time as any."

Outside, she suggested, "You go to the left. I'll catch him up on this side."

Evan's eyes were wide and alert, like a threatened animal's, as he spotted his sisters closing in. "What are you two doing here?" he stammered.

Kelly saw no reason to delay. They might as well move in for the kill, while he was still suffering from the shock of being ensnared.

"I don't suppose," Kelly teased, "I imagined an MI5-style exchange of cheese and onion crisps, did I?"

Evan blinked at her, then said, "I don't know what you mean."

Lowering her voice, Kelly asked, "Could it be that you put some money in your crisp packet so the fella with the blue Peugeot could take it without anyone knowing? Then, after he'd checked it, he handed something to you in return, using the same trick." She paused, then added, "You're not into drugs, are you?"

"Drugs?" he exclaimed. "You've got to be . . ." His eyes flitted around. Outside the club several youngsters were drifting like lost souls. He didn't want them to overhear, so he replied, "I'm not saying anything. Not here."

"Let's go for a walk then," Kelly suggested.

They crossed the road and took the path that skirted round the artificial lake. On a windy day, the lake would be packed with sailboards, like colourful sharks' fins. Now, in the gloom of early evening, it was calm and still. The ducks reclaimed the water and paddled in safety, looking for food. The wind surfers were probably confined to the pub on the other side of the lake.

"Come on," Sarah said. "Let's have the truth."

"The truth?"

"Yes," Kelly added. "If you don't, we'll use our own imagination – and we'll probably imagine something much worse than it really is."

"You already have." Evan stopped walking and leaned on a fence overlooking the lake. Keeping his gaze on the lighted windows of the pub, he mumbled, "You've got it all wrong. It's nothing serious."

"What is it then?" Kelly persisted.

Unwillingly, Evan murmured, "Sometimes it's soccer scores. Sometimes horses. It's even been ice-skating."

"What has?" Sarah asked, bemused.

"I put a bit of money on the results," he admitted.

"Gambling!" Kelly surmised.

Evan nodded.

"I get it!" said Kelly. "You checked out the horses on the screen, then you told that bloke what you're backing while he took your money, disguised in a crisp packet, and gave you . . . what? Some sort of receipt?"

"A betting slip. Prints out a proper record on a computer – probably in his car."

"He *is* well organized, isn't he?" Kelly exclaimed in exasperation. "But one thing's for sure – it's against the law. He won't have a licence or whatever."

"No," Evan confessed. "It's not exactly above board."

"When you say, 'a bit of money', what do you mean?" Sarah added.

Evan blushed. "Not much. And I win some-times."

"How much did you just lose?"

Evan mumbled, "He takes a fiver as a minimum bet."

Sarah cursed.

"You lost a fiver – or more – just like that? Evan!"

"You sound just like Mum sometimes," he countered.

Kelly didn't have time to be stung by his comment. Her thoughts had raced ahead. "I'm beginning to understand," she said. "That morning, Friday the thirteenth, Mum found out about this gambling business didn't she? You had a row about it."

Evan nodded again. "Found a betting slip in my trousers."

Suddenly it became clear to Kelly. "Dinner Date! They give horses daft names. Did you bet on a horse called Dinner Date?"

"It came in second," he admitted.

"The ten and the six?" queried Sarah.

"A tenner at six to one," Evan answered.

"Ah." The Keating sisters nodded knowingly at each other. "I see now," Kelly declared. "You couldn't tell the police you were really arguing about gambling because it's not legal at your age. Thought they'd do you for it. They'd do that bloke inside as well – preying on youngsters. Anyway," she continued, "when you'd finished arguing with Mum, she took the slip off you. That's how come it was in her bag."

"Yes," Evan whispered.

"It's obvious, then," Sarah commented.

"What is?"

"Mum and this boyfriend. They met to talk over what she should do to stop this little earner. Somehow, that bloke inside found out and . . . put an end to it. First Mum, then McCormick."

"He did get into a Peugeot 405," Kelly added, "so it might fit. But right now, what are we going to do about you, Evan?"

"Me? What do you mean?"

"I'm worried about you. It may not be as bad as drugs, but you've got to stop."

"Why? It's my money."

"Because it's almost as addictive as drugs. And you never know what it can lead to. Debts. Thieving to support the habit. That sort of thing."

"I know," Evan muttered unconvincingly.

"So, do you reckon you can stop?"

"Sure," he responded in a tone midway between confidence and indifference. "I' could quit any time."

"Why do you do it, Evan?" Kelly queried.

He shrugged. "The adrenalin, I suppose. You get really high during a race. You wouldn't understand if you haven't done it."

"Perhaps not. It just seems like a waste of money to me. Still, I've done enough preaching. I don't suppose any more will help."

Evan looked away.

After a pause, Sarah asked, "What's that man's name?"

"No idea," Evan replied. "Everyone calls him Pete, that's all."

"Pete," Sarah repeated. "That's the one."

Kelly nodded slowly, thoughtfully. "Could be," she murmured.

In front of them, a duck upended itself. As it probed unseen in the mud at the bottom, its backside wobbled comically in the air.

"We're going to have to dig up some dirt on him," she concluded. "Does he always hang about in Revolvers?"

"Weekends and most nights, yes. They pipe in a sports channel all the time so it's convenient enough for him. Sometimes he does other places. He arranges afternoon betting parties now and again."

"Have you been bunking off school?" Sarah asked.

"Not much," Evan muttered.

Kelly sighed. "And you wanted to know why you should stop! You're hooked!"

"What about Thursday nights?" Sarah questioned. "The night McCormick copped it."

"He used to meet clients down beside the canal, under the old bridge, before taking them to a gambling den. Now they're building a new bridge, he puts in another night at Revolvers instead."

"Did you see him on Thursday?" Kelly continued. "That would give him an alibi."

"No," Evan replied. "I was somewhere else."

"So," Kelly concluded, "he's got to go on our hit list. I think we'll have to do something about him."

"You can't mess with him, Kelly," Sarah warned. "Seriously. He's probably raking it in. He'd go a long way to protect his interests. Maybe he has already."

"So," her sister asked, "what do you think we should do?"

Sarah breathed in deeply, then shrugged. "I don't know. Turn him in to the police for running an illegal gambling business?"

"That won't help with the murder," Kelly commented.

A car roared into life in the car park beside the pub, and cast two parallel beams across the water. As it pulled away, the beams swept over the lake as if searching out waterfowl.

"How are you going to prove it was him?" asked Sarah. "Put him under a spotlight and interrogate him?"

Kelly grinned at her sister. "No, I wasn't thinking of that."

"What then?"

It was Kelly's turn to look helpless, but only for a moment. Her face brightened and she turned to Evan. "Has your Pete got a proper job, do you know?"

"Not sure," he answered. "Someone told me he had something to do with the building trade."

"Ah! He doesn't work for Henderson's, does he?"

"I don't know."

Even Sarah had to admit that they had a lead now. "We could ask Mr Henderson if he employed this Pete for the video factory."

"How?" Kelly asked. "Half his builders are probably called Pete, and we can hardly say Pete the bookie."

"I suppose not."

Kelly tilted her head to one side as she thought about it for a moment. "What we need," she proclaimed, "is a photo of him. Then we could take it to Mr Henderson."

Sarah took up the logic eagerly. "And if he identifies Pete as one of his crew, that'll just about sew it up. This Pete would have the motive *and* it'd come naturally to him to . . ." Her voice lost its fire as she finished the sentence, "To get rid of a body . . . like that."

"Why wait six months before going after McCormick?" Kelly wondered aloud. Then, answering her own question, she said, "Perhaps Pete was checking out our family. He'd have to have done that to concoct that suicide note." Turning to Evan, she inquired, "Has he ever asked you about Mum and Dad?"

"Hardly said anything to me. Or me to him."

"He could have been snooping without us knowing about it," Sarah put in.

"Yes," Kelly agreed. "Or maybe McCormick was snooping on *him*. Doing a bit of research, getting evidence, before telling his wife all about him. If McCormick got a bit too close – curtains."

"So," Sarah insisted, "it *is* risky to mess with him."

"It's Sunday tomorrow. He'll be back here at the centre. I reckon I can snap him without him even knowing. It shouldn't be too difficult, with Evan's help."

Both sisters turned towards Evan. He looked at them, then turned away, pretending to be interested in a passing moorhen. After a few seconds of silence, he shook his head dejectedly. "All right," he murmured. "What do you want me to do?"

8

The three Keatings each chipped in some money. They changed it into a ten-pound note and Evan folded it to the size of a postage stamp and slipped it into a small sheath. "That," he said to his sisters, "goes into the crisp packet. He'll take it with a few crisps."

"Hope he doesn't swallow it," Kelly quipped, despite her tingling nerves. "He'd have a bit of a wait before he got his money back."

"Have you got your camera?" Sarah asked.

"It's in the bag," Kelly replied, tapping her handbag. "So let's get cracking."

The girls went into Revolvers first. Fifteen minutes later, Evan strolled in, bought a packet of crisps and sat down two tables away. As instructed, he did not even glance at them. He sat and scratched the top of his head, which was the signal that he wanted to place a bet with Pete. Then he chewed his fingernails mercilessly as he studied the list of runners for the heats of a 5,000-metre race at some athletics event.

Kelly used Pete's first approach to Evan to gauge the angles, then manoeuvred herself into what she thought was the right position, ready for his return. She hoped her hand wouldn't shake too much to get a decent photo when he passed the betting slip to her brother.

The three of them waited tensely. Kelly checked the camera setting for the third time.

Sarah's eyes darted to the entrance and nervously her lips formed the words, "He's coming."

Just as Pete hesitated by Evan, bent down and offered him a smoky bacon crisp, Kelly clicked the button. There was a flash. Pete straightened up. Anger and panic were clear on his face even in the semi-darkness. All he saw was a young woman beckoning to her sister and yelling, "Stand up! I'll take another like that. Hold your drink up!"

Sarah yanked her fingers out of her hair and got to her feet. Lifting her glass towards the camera, she mouthed, "Cheers!"

There was a second flash.

Pete relaxed a little but moved away as quickly as he could.

Kelly had taken a photograph of Pete, then turned rapidly and directed the camera at Sarah. Pete had not looked up in time to see the change of angle. He was unaware that his image had been captured on film.

The girls plonked themselves down into their seats and sighed. It took a few seconds before they were capable of smiling at each other, and almost a minute before they stopped trembling. Then Kelly put her thumb up and Sarah lip-read her message, "Got it."

They waited for twenty minutes before they left the club, shortly after Evan's departure. The race had finished and he had lost again. Kelly was driving her dad's car and she pulled up at the end of the street to let Evan get in.

"Well done," she congratulated him. "It worked. It's in the can, as they say."

In the scruffy reception of Henderson's Builders, Kelly's eyebrows rose. "Faye!" she cried.

"Kelly!" the secretary replied.

They had been at school together. Kelly had stayed on, Faye had left at sixteen. She'd married, had one kid, and got divorced, all within two years. Now she just about supported herself and her boy by working part-time as Mrs Keating's replacement at Henderson's while a friend took care of the baby.

"What are you doing here?" Faye asked.

"Just . . . er . . . some unfinished business with your boss. Do you think we can see him?"

Sarah stood beside her sister and Evan cowered behind. They'd managed to drag him along because he knew Pete better than they did.

"I suppose so," Faye replied. "He hasn't got anyone with him at the moment." She rose and headed towards Mr Henderson's door.

Kelly caught her arm. "Thanks. But first, why don't we get together again? Say tonight?"

"That'd be nice," Faye answered. "But it's difficult. You know, with the baby." She looked disappointed.

"You could come to our place," Kelly offered. "Bring the baby."

"Well . . ." Faye had always been a bit scatty and indecisive. "I don't know."

"Tell you what," Kelly said to encourage her, "I'll pick you up and drive you across. No problem."

The smile was a long time coming to Faye's attractive but worn face. Eventually she nodded. "Okay. I'll jot my address down and give you it before you go."

Kelly and Sarah returned her smile.

There weren't enough chairs for them all to sit in Eric Henderson's office so Kelly took the seat in front of his desk and the other two stood behind her like bodyguards. Mr Henderson wore an expression of curiosity and surprise. He had a big bushy beard that gave his face a comical appearance. None of the Keatings was fooled by this impression. His manner and the hardness of his eyes suggested a ruthless businessman.

He cocked his head on one side and said, "I agreed to see you out of respect for your mother. What do you want?"

Kelly had rehearsed her piece in the car on the way to Henderson's. "We're concerned about a loose end in the investigation into Mum's death. We have reason to believe that this man," she held out the recently developed photograph, "might hold the key."

Eric Henderson still looked puzzled. Barely glancing at the photo, he asked, "What do you mean? What sort of key?"

Kelly had hoped he wouldn't quiz her along those lines. "We think he might have been with Mum just before she died."

"Look," Mr Henderson replied, "it's over. George McCormick couldn't take rejection, it seems. Simple as that. I lost two good employees and you lost a mother. Let's leave it at that."

"But this man," Kelly persisted, "might have been in on it. We want to get to the truth. His name's Pete. Do you know him?"

"Why should I?"

"Because he's a builder," Sarah put in.

On the other side of the desk, Henderson sighed heavily and examined the photograph. Pete was bending over Evan so it had not caught his full face, but there was enough: a stocky man in his twenties with cropped mousy hair, a broken nose and thick eyebrows.

Henderson laid the photo on his desk and looked into Kelly's eyes. "If you think he's one of my men, you probably think he worked on the video factory. That means you think he was involved in killing your mother – or at least in getting rid of the body."

Kelly nodded. "Well?"

He returned the photograph. "Sorry, he's not one of mine."

Kelly wanted to look away but forced herself to keep her eyes on Eric Henderson's face. There was a silence as she gazed at him, assessing his character. He was obviously annoyed to have his time disrupted by kids who were trying to dredge up an old relic that should be allowed to rest, but his reply was direct and sincere. She thought he was probably telling the truth. "Okay," she said, reclaiming the photograph and standing up. "We won't bother you any more."

Before they shuffled out of the door and returned to the reception area, Mr Henderson called after them, "There's been enough tragedy. Let your mum rest in peace."

*   *   *

Back inside the borrowed car, Evan finally spoke. "What about showing the photo at that seafood place? In case the owner saw Pete hanging around that Friday while Mum was inside."

His interest took his sisters by surprise. They both turned in their seats and peered at him. "That's a good idea," Kelly declared. "If they'll speak to us."

Evan did not reply. He had lapsed into disinterested silence again.

The visit to The Seafood Spree turned out to be a waste of time. They did get to see Daniel Perriman but his shallow smile soon faded when it became clear that the party of three was not Tuesday evening's first group of customers. In fact, when he realized their true mission, he turned out to be rather grumpy.

"Look," he snapped. "This death has brought me enough bad publicity what with police visits and everything. I've done my bit. I answered their questions and identified a body. Now I've put it all behind me. I'm a caterer, not a crook."

"Just a quick look," Kelly said softly. "It won't hurt, surely."

Grudgingly, the man put on his spectacles and glanced at the photo. He did not even take it out of Kelly's hand.

"No," he said impatiently. "I've never seen him. And now," he added, pushing his way to the door and opening it, "I bid you goodbye."

"Thanks, anyway," Kelly muttered on the way out.

"I don't know why you thanked him," Sarah commented. "He almost said no before he looked."

"I know," Kelly replied. "Just my upbringing, I suppose."

The third person to examine Kelly's photograph that day was Faye. She held baby James on her knee with one hand and the photo in the other.

"Mr Henderson said he'd never seen him, but have you?" Kelly prompted.

"Don't know," Faye replied. A few more moments of consideration brought a more definite response. "No," she said. "There's someone at work quite like him but no, it's definitely not him. This bloke's not been around while I've been there." She handed back the photo.

"All right," Kelly conceded. Changing the subject, she asked, "Do you like it at Henderson's?"

Faye shrugged. "It's a job." She seemed reluctant to show any enthusiasm and her cheeks reddened.

"It's all right," Kelly said. "You don't have to be embarrassed about replacing Mum. It wasn't your fault."

"Yeah. But . . ." She fiddled with the baby's clothes rather than finish the sentence.

"It's not going so well, I understand. Not much building work."

"True. That's the reason I got the job, I reckon. I'm not a fast typist and I'm not the most organized, but he doesn't have to pay me as much as someone experienced like . . ."

"Like Mum."

Faye nodded. "He has to cut corners to survive. I only do two days a week. It just about keeps us going, me and the baby." She jogged him on her knee.

Kelly wondered whether Henderson's predicament had anything to do with her mum's fate. The two murders had become so prominent in her mind that she scrutinized everything people said for relevance but she could not make any connections here.

"Did you know Mr McCormick?" she asked. "The one who . . . killed himself?"

Faye squirmed uncomfortably in her seat. "George? Yes," she said glumly. "I wasn't surprised, mind. He wasn't the life and soul of any party. Miserable, he was, but angry as well. I can't honestly say I liked him, but I'm sorry he . . . you know."

"He didn't happen to ask you about this man, did he?" Kelly waved the photograph in the air.

"No. Didn't ask me anything other than normal work stuff – you know, wanted this or that file, or a bit of typing."

They chatted for a while longer but the evening

petered out. Faye wasn't a good talker and, with the baby to occupy her, she wasn't a good listener either. When Kelly gave her a lift home, they vowed to keep in touch. In Kelly's case, politeness demanded it. For Faye, the evening had been a real break from her daily routine. She had enjoyed the evening and was grateful to her friend for suggesting it. She was looking forward to a repeat performance.

On Wednesday, Kelly and Sarah stood in the doorway of Evan's bedroom like a nervous double act on a ludicrously small stage.

"You're in tonight," Sarah stated.

"No. I've just come on in the last five minutes to score the winning goal at Wembley," Evan replied with a blank expression. He could have been indulging in ridicule or humour; it was impossible to say.

"What she means," Kelly put in, "is that we're pleased you're staying in."

"Oh." He didn't need to ask why. His sisters knew that if he stayed at home, avoiding Pete, he couldn't gamble. And that would please them because they had begun a crusade to get him to kick the habit.

Evan's craving for excitement had started when he first realized that his mum had found a lover. The exact reason for turning to gambling was never clear in his own mind. In spite of what he'd told the police, he thought he might have been responsible for his mother's need for someone else. The thrill of the race and the high stakes helped him to forget the guilt. At times he knew it wasn't his fault and he just felt angry with her, but he kept a lid on his resentment. Instead of proclaiming his fury from the roof-tops, he discovered that he could punish her by turning to something outside the family.

Because his mum forced him to play second fiddle to some boyfriend, Evan made her the poor relation to his gambling. Now, there was little point in punishing the dead, so he saw the sense of his sisters' crusade. He would try to live without the element of risk, without abandoning himself to luck, without the elation of winning. Besides, he didn't relish another meeting with Pete, in case he realized that there had been a conspiracy against him. On top of that, Evan no longer had the cash.

"It struck me," Kelly continued, "that betting's an expensive business, even if you did win now and again. How did you afford it?"

Evan noted her use of the past tense but didn't object. "Paper round. And pocket money. That sort of thing."

"But . . . er . . . surely that wasn't enough."

Evan's head drooped as he hesitated. He'd never told anyone about his other way of making money.

"You see," Kelly explained, "we've put Pete the bookie on our list of suspects but we've come to the end of the road with him – for the moment. We were wondering if there was anything else we should know about." She took up a position on her brother's bed as he nodded.

"I suppose I might as well tell you now," he mumbled. "I didn't tell anyone before because I needed the cash. I couldn't risk letting on about the videos, or the source of money would've dried up."

"What do you mean?" Sarah inquired.

"I didn't want Mr Warr taken away for murder, did I?"

"Why should he be?"

"Because someone at Mum's work told her they'd seen me in . . . one of his videos."

"*What?*" Kelly exploded.

"Sometimes I did a bit of work for Mr Warr. His proper business – distributing videos – is legit, of course, but he runs a scam on the side. That's how he funded the extension. A racket in making videos."

"Don't tell me you starred in some of them!"

"No, not really," Evan stammered. Then he conceded, "Well, yes. A bit."

"A bit?" Sarah cried. "Either you did or you didn't."

"He's got a studio where he makes the films. I

91

help out, lugging props around the place – that sort of thing. But sometimes, if he needs a crowd or a passer-by, he gets me to join in. It's not really acting, it's just being there."

Kelly sighed. "Let me get this straight. You earned a bit on the side by helping Mr Warr make these videos. What sort of videos are we talking about, Evan? Why aren't they legitimate?"

"It's not what you think. They're okay videos – more or less. Just cheap. A bit of horror, science fiction, supernatural – anything that can be done in a studio and put together on a shoestring. It's the type of operation that the tax office doesn't get to hear about. Struggling actors, moonlighting un-employed – he uses those sorts of people. Ones that need some cash in their pockets without all the complications of national insurance, tax and stuff."

"He uses underage kids as well," Sarah remarked irritably. "It's called slave labour." She seemed to have developed an instant dislike for Mr Warr and his dealings. It didn't help that she couldn't forget the unhappiness he had caused her mother when the planning permission row was in full swing.

"Yeah. I put in more hours than I'm supposed to. I did quite a few nights and weekends. Took a bit of time off school as well. But I had to – for the pay."

"That's bad enough, but isn't there a law about

schoolkids performing in films? Doesn't Warr need some sort of licence?" Kelly checked.

"I think so," Evan answered. "But . . . er . . ."

"He didn't bother with that either," Kelly deduced. "Some racket! You only mix with the best, don't you? Pete the bookie and now Warr. Anyway," she said, "someone at Mum's work saw one of the videos and spotted you – passing by or whatever. Told Mum what you were up to. Then she had that row with you. Have we finally heard what it was really about, that argument? You doing this video stuff to fund the gambling?"

Her brother nodded.

"And you didn't tell us or the police because you'd lose the job," Sarah deduced. "And the income that went with it."

"Yes."

"This is important," Kelly put in. "After that row, Mum could have threatened to expose Warr – to stop your little game. To stop *her*, he might have killed her."

"Yes," Evan agreed in a subdued voice. "I know. I think he did it. I phoned him about it, you know."

"You accused him of murder?" Sarah exclaimed.

"Nearly. He denied it, of course."

The three of them fell silent for a moment, then Kelly murmured, "Is that the lot? You haven't got any more nasty surprises for us, have you?"

"No," he replied. "You know it all now."

"Well, what do we do? Warr looks like a real suspect, suddenly. He could've easily put the body in the wall. And he might have had a go at Mr McCormick as well if he'd been poking his nose in, trying to get evidence on Warr's racket."

"And now you want us to snoop on him too," Sarah moaned.

Kelly shrugged. "Let's hear some better ideas," she said.

She didn't get any.

Admitting defeat, Sarah asked, "What have you got in mind? A raid on his wardrobe for a green jumper?"

"No. But we could check out his car, at least. Do you know what he's got, Evan?"

"Something big and showy, like a Daimler, I think."

"Not a Peugeot?"

"Not that I know of. But he's rich. He's probably got more than one."

"And *have* you ever seen him in a green jumper?"

Evan looked blank.

"Evan's a boy," Sarah put in. "Boys never notice clothes."

"I don't suppose you were working for him on the night Mum died, were you?" Kelly asked.

Evan shook his head. "I was at Revolvers, I'm

afraid. Waited around all night but Pete didn't show. I can't rule either of them out."

Changing the subject so that none of them had to dwell on that evening, Kelly murmured, "What about last Thursday? I'd like to know what Warr was doing that night as well." Looking at Evan, she inquired, "You didn't call him then, did you?"

"No. It was before that. But," Evan added, "I think I know someone who could help. Someone called John."

"What are we waiting for?" Kelly commented.

"Because John's . . . Well, you'll see what he's like. Just don't be put off. He's okay really."

They found John in a dingy sports club. He was clinging to the ropes of the boxing ring and shouting childlike encouragement to whichever combatant seemed to be getting the worst of it. Unlike Kelly and Sarah, he did not wince each time a punch thudded home. He was built like Humpty Dumpty with muscles – or a Mr Universe pumped up like a balloon. His layer of fat made him look much older than he probably was, but his chubby face was soft and young. It was a face that could never be clouded by unhappiness.

"Evan!" he called when he caught sight of his friend. Letting go of the ropes, he waddled across the room, dodging the medicine balls and table tennis tables, with a baby's exaggerated expression of joy on his face. "How're you doing, old son?"

"All right, John. You?"

"You know me," he chimed. Turning to Kelly and Sarah as if he'd known them from birth, he said, "Last time I seen Evan, he was covered in blood! Heh, heh, heh!" His laugh could have brought all the activities in the hall to a stop, but the punters were used to him. "Remember?" he chortled.

Evan could hardly forget. He had been in charge of a knife attached to a tube that delivered red liquid to the plastic blade when it apparently bit into flesh – a standard prop for a horror film. That day, though, he had applied too great a pressure to the liquid and when it was pumped through, the knife leapt out of the actress's hand and snaked, like an out-of-control hose-pipe, spurting fake blood everywhere – over the actress, who howled with laughter; over Evan, who was too shocked to see the funny side of it; over Warr; over John and the rest.

"Yes," Evan muttered. "I remember."

"Explosion in a red paint factory," John giggled. "The bread knife massacre! Great stuff. Anyway, I ain't seen you much these days."

"Keeping a low profile," Evan replied. "Are you still doing work for Mr Warr?"

"Sure am. Went quiet, it did, while he got the factory sorted. Now he's started up again. Still likes me, he do."

It wasn't true, of course. Evan knew that the film-maker did not so much like John as take advantage of him. Whenever some heavy scenery needed shifting, John provided the muscle. He'd even performed a few feats of strength on film, but he wasn't an aggressive type. He once got a job as a bouncer at a night club because he looked like a man who could move mountains, but two weeks later he got the sack because he couldn't bring himself to harm a fly.

It also occurred to Evan that, if the studio was back in action but he hadn't been asked to take part, Warr must be avoiding him. In Warr's eyes, Evan had probably been tainted by his contact with the police. It would be too dangerous to give him any more work, despite what he'd said to Evan on the telephone.

John beamed at Sarah and invited her to feel his biceps. She patted the enormous mound of flesh and muscle in his upper arm and, with as much admiration as she could muster, murmured, "Mmm!"

"Good, eh? Good for lifting tree trunks!" Seeing an expression of disbelief beginning to form on Sarah's face, he added quickly, "In films, like. Not really." His chuckle almost made the earth move.

"Making a new video, is he?" Evan asked.

"Yep," John replied. "Haunted house or something."

"What is it? Filming just at weekends, or on week days?"

"Behind schedule, he says, after the wall collapsed." He laughed again, not thinking of what it might mean to the Keatings, then continued, "So we're at it most afternoons and nights."

"Like last Thursday?"

"Last Thursday?" John repeated. "That were years ago," he cried happily. "Let me think."

Evan caught an errant table tennis ball and threw it back to one of the players while they waited for John's brain to tick over like an unwilling engine on a winter's morning.

"Yes," he pronounced eventually. "Thursday. One of the girls, she were going on about seeing some group on *Top of the Pops*. Great, she said they were. That's Thursdays, ain't it?"

"Yes," Evan answered. "And was Mr Warr at the shoot?"

"Sure."

Sarah looked disappointed. She would have dearly loved to nail Warr for murder.

"All the time?" Evan asked.

"I don't know," John replied. "He . . . er . . . No. The producer were cursing him at some point. Heh, heh! Couldn't get on. Wanted Mr Warr to decide on something but he'd scarpered early, like."

The Keatings glanced at each other triumphantly.

"What time would that be, John?"

"It's no use asking me about time," he sniggered. "Never notice it. Eight? Nine? I don't know."

"Okay. Never mind. Just one more thing," Evan said. "You've done stuff with him for ages, haven't you?"

"Yep! He knows good prime beef when he sees it. Always wanted me on the set. A film star, me."

"You've probably seen him driving around a bit. You know that big car he's got?"

"Mercedes. Cracking set of wheels."

Evan nodded. "Ever seen him in another car? Ages ago, maybe."

"Er ..." John scratched his head with stodgy fingers. "He's had a VW, I think. And a Peugeot."

"A Peugeot?"

"Yes. Sure. Red, it were."

Evan grinned at him. "Thanks," he said.

"Are you off now?"

The Keatings nodded.

"Pity," John said. "Still, maybe you'll come in and help out soon, eh?"

Evan returned his smile. "Maybe," he said. "Look after yourself, John."

"Sure will!"

Outside the club, Sarah was furious. "It makes me so angry!" she bawled. "He's just a ... big buffoon. And Warr's taking advantage of him."

"He didn't even ask why we wanted to know all

those things," Kelly said, agreeing with her sister. "He's in another world, the poor chap."

"I know," Evan said. "But it's only the filming that allows him to make a living. You've got to give it that."

"I know what I'd like to give it," Sarah cried.

"It's time to do something about this Warr," Kelly added. "He could be our man. He might have control over life and death in his films, but not in real life."

Sarah agreed. "He deserves everything he's got coming to him."

"Like what?" Evan pondered.

"We'll flush him out into the open," Kelly replied.

"What do you mean?" asked Sarah.

"Well," Kelly explained as she opened the car doors and they all piled in, "what was his motive for murder?"

Sarah shrugged. "Mum threatened to expose his illegal filming. McCormick probably found some evidence to take to the police, so he copped it as well." She hesitated, glancing at her sister. "Oh, no! You're not thinking of threatening him ourselves!"

"Why not?"

"Because we'd be dead meat."

"How else are we going to flush him out?" Kelly argued. "Besides, I know how we can confront him *and* be safe while we're doing it."

"Oh yes?"

"It's a nice irony. We meet him at the centre of the indoor market," she proposed. "You know, where there's seats."

"Where's the irony in that?" Sarah asked her.

"It's monitored by video, remember? To catch shoplifters or whatever. He can't do anything to us – he'll be under surveillance at the time. It'll all be on video."

"And when we leave the market?" Sarah queried. "The cameras don't follow you home, you know."

"We'll just have to be careful."

9

The circular market was a colossal concrete cake in the centre of the town, constructed in the boom years when buildings were big, bold blots on the landscape. In those days, there was enough money around for Henderson's to build it solidly, like an impregnable fortress. By the time its bad architectural style had been recognized, it would have cost another fortune to knock it down and start again. With money in short supply, the blemish was likely to stand till doomsday.

Inside, the stalls were arranged in rings. Customers could walk round and round for ever. Newcomers were easy to spot. They negotiated the market like a maze: they knew roughly where they had entered, but weren't sure where they wanted to go or how to get there, and they ended up shuffling round in a state of bewilderment.

After school on Friday, Kelly, Sarah and Evan strode past the lost souls and converged rapidly on the hub of the market. There, seats and tables were laid out and drinks and hot dogs were being served from a kiosk. They each bought themselves a coffee and then sat at one of the tables, glancing nervously towards the shoppers who circled them. Waiting for Warr to emerge from the crowds, they felt exposed, expecting a solitary and dangerous predator to come at them from any angle like a shark.

"He'll make for you," Kelly said to Evan, "because he doesn't know me or Sarah."

"Yes." Evan looked at his watch. "Nearly four," he muttered.

By telephone, Evan had persuaded Warr to agree to meet them in the market at four o'clock. Warr's resistance towards the meeting had been broken down once Evan had convinced him that he had no further desire to take part in his illegal videos. With that decision, Evan had become a threat in Warr's eyes and had to be taken seriously. The boy could blab to the police if he no longer lived in fear of losing the considerable amount he earned through backstreet filming. If Evan really could do without the money, Warr had lost his hold over him. The whole operation was in jeopardy because of an out-of-control and underage ex-member of his underground crew.

Above their table in the market, among the dangling strip lights, there hung a small dome with four camera lenses aiming in different directions. In the centre of the dome, a red light flashed on and off to bring shoppers' attention to the video surveillance.

When Warr finally stepped into the arena at four-fifteen, he was turned out immaculately. Even though Kelly and Sarah had never seen him before, they recognized him immediately. In such a down-beat place, he was like a fish out of water. Sarah nudged her sister and whispered, "Bet that's him. Very posh."

"Yeah," Kelly replied. "Remember, not all villains look like scarecrows and wear stockings over their heads."

Behind the carefully preened exterior, Warr's face suggested a worried man. Taking a seat opposite Evan, he nodded towards Kelly and Sarah and declared, "I didn't expect an audience."

"My sisters," Evan retorted.

"Yes," Warr snapped. "I can see the resemblance. But what I want to know is, what do they know?"

Kelly interjected, "We're not dumb. We can speak for ourselves. And Evan's told us everything."

Warr unbuttoned his jacket slowly. "I see." Still not addressing Kelly or Sarah, he looked at Evan and remarked, "I suppose they made you change your mind about working for me."

Sarah was about to comment that Evan could stand on his own two feet, but she stopped herself. If it was true, she'd better let him at least speak for himself.

"Maybe," Evan grumbled. Then, looking straight at Warr, he added, "But I think I'm entitled to change. What with Mum's body falling in front of me and all."

Warr regarded Evan intently for a moment before replying, "I suppose so." He levered himself into a more comfortable position in the plastic seat. "So why not just disappear from the scene? You didn't have to call me."

"Because we know all about you," Evan responded.

"What's that supposed to mean?" asked Warr. "Is it money you're after? A golden handshake?"

"No," Kelly blurted out.

"What then?" he said, peering at the girls this time.

"Our mum was driven around in a Peugeot before she was killed. You had a Peugeot. Her body was dumped at your building site. You'd know all about that—"

Warr interrupted. "Not again!" He gave a loud but hollow laugh. "You want me to break down and confess to a murder. I don't believe it. Three kids! You have to be joking! It was absurd enough when Evan tried to blame me over the phone. Listen. Let me spell it out for you. I had nothing to do with . . ." He leaned forward and lowered his voice, but it still retained its harshness. ". . . with your mother's death. Why should I?"

"Because she heard about Evan working on your videos. We think she had a go at you for it. Probably threatened you. Plenty of motive."

"But—"

Before he could defend himself, Sarah exclaimed, "And there's last Thursday night."

"What about it?" Warr queried, agitatedly.

Evan explained that, despite the police's suicide verdict, they believed his mum's boyfriend had been murdered on that night, presumably after he'd investigated her death.

"But . . . how many times do I have to say it? Your mum didn't approach me about the videos. I hadn't got a clue that she was seeing another man, and why would I want to kill him?"

"You would if he threatened you as well. You know all about murder," Sarah said, scratching her arm nervously. "You've staged it in films."

"Yes. True. But let's not confuse fact and fiction. If this boyfriend was murdered and you say it was made to look like suicide, that requires skill. It's not easy to fool police pathologists, you know. You should be looking for a real expert."

Kelly plucked up enough courage to reply, "We don't believe you. Unless you've got an alibi for Thursday night."

The factory owner hesitated and then sneered at them. "As a matter of fact, I have." Keeping his voice to a whisper, he explained, "I was on a set last Thursday, filming."

"The whole evening?"

"Yes."

"Well, we have information that you left early."

Warr's eyes opened wide with surprise. "You what?"

"You heard."

Recovering as if from a blow, he shrugged like a boxer pretending he hadn't been hurt. "I don't have to answer to you."

"No," Kelly replied, "but you'll have to answer to the police."

"You're going to tell them?"

The three Keatings nodded.

"You'll make fools of yourselves," Warr said to his accusers. "On Thursday, I went out for a meal – with a young lady acquaintance." He seemed proud of his liaison with her.

"Not The Seafood Spree," Sarah blurted out.

Mr Warr looked surprised at her comment. "No. A Chinese meal, actually."

"Well, you *would* say you were somewhere else

with someone else, wouldn't you?" Sarah said, still hostile towards him.

"I wouldn't want to give the police her name, but I will if I have to – to clear my name."

"So you get a friend to swear blind that she was with you. Not very convincing."

"Look," Warr said, banging his fist on the table so that Evan's empty polystyrene cup fell over, "I'm not an unreasonable man. I can see why you think I might have . . . had it in for your mother. We weren't the best of friends. And you three are desperate to find someone to blame. But there's no need to get paranoid about it."

"We're not," Sarah declared. "It all fits and you deserve—"

"Just a minute," Warr interrupted. "It all fits, you say. But does it?" He suddenly looked pleased with himself. He adjusted his bright flowery tie to make his audience wait and wonder. "Your mum heard about the videos. That's what you claim. As a result, she came after my blood. But you're forgetting something. Did you tell her *I* made the videos?" Looking directly into Evan's face, he added, "Did you say to her, 'Trevor Warr did the filming'? I doubt it. Not if you valued your earnings from me. I'd hazard a guess that my name was never mentioned."

"I . . . er . . ." Evan blushed.

"Well? Did you tell her?"

"I can't remember. It was nearly six months ago," Evan muttered.

"You'd better think about it, my lad," Warr said, rising to his feet and wiping his hands together as if to remove the grime of the market-place. "Because if you didn't tell her, she'd hardly come pounding on my door. She wouldn't know it was me. And," he added, wagging a finger unpleasantly, "before I leave you with that thought, rest assured that if any of you talk to the police about this, or about my video work, you'll regret it." He swanked away from the table and vanished among the mass of bargain hunters.

Kelly and Sarah sat stunned, staring at Evan, with the same word on their lips. "Well?"

Evan looked at them and shook his head. "I don't think I did . . . but she heard about the video at work. Whoever told her might have known Warr was behind it."

His sisters looked doubtful but were keen to clutch at straws. Sarah nodded and murmured, "Possibly."

"Yes," Kelly agreed. "Or we might have got carried away a bit because – let's face it – we don't like him because he exploits people like Evan and John."

"But there's evidence as well," Sarah objected.

"True, but he doesn't look the green jumper type."

"I wouldn't put it past him to have a green suit," Sarah retorted.

Kelly sighed. "I reckon we've got to think again. He might have done it but – like Pete the bookie – we'll have to park the idea for a bit. Unless we get any more info." They got up and trudged dismally out of the maze.

On the way home, Kelly kept thinking about something that Warr had said to them: "You should be looking for a real expert." His words haunted her. Perhaps he had a point, she thought. And on her list of suspects, she had only one expert in police work.

10

It was Faye who provided Kelly with some unexpected clues. At her request, they met at the Keatings' house again on Saturday afternoon. Evan was absorbed in the sport on television and baby James tottered round the room, investigating everything, falling over and screaming at regular intervals. Clive Keating was minding the shop and Sarah, conscious that she'd been neglecting her boyfriend lately, was out with Matt.

"That photo you showed us," Faye said.

"Yes?" Kelly replied, trying to goad a more useful statement from her guest.

"Well, it's been on my mind," she began. "You know I said there was someone at work who looked a bit like the fella in your picture? Roger. I took more notice of him after I seen you last and . . . er . . . outside the yard, I think Roger met the chap in the photo."

Kelly sat erect and attentive and Evan turned his head away from the television. Then James tripped over a chair leg and cried as if his entire world had been shattered. Kelly had to wait till his mother had picked him up and calmed him down before the conversation could be resumed.

"I seen him in a car. Well, he was standing by it. Waiting, at going home time, to pick up Roger. When I seen them together, they looked like brothers. Perhaps they are."

Trying not to get too excited, Kelly asked, "Was it a Peugeot? Blue?"

"I didn't notice it much. It could've been. But, yeah, it was blue."

"What about this Roger? What does he do?" Kelly queried, with the fingers of both hands crossed.

"He's one of the builders."

"And did he work on the extension to the video factory?"

Faye turned her attention momentarily to James. "Better? Want to go walkies again?" She lifted him down to the floor. Looking at Kelly, she answered, "Yes. Roger would've done that job."

Kelly's sigh was almost audible. She uncrossed her fingers. Suddenly, Pete was back in the frame in a big way. He certainly would have had a motive if her mum had tried to intervene in his gambling scam. Now, it transpired that, through his brother, he would have had the knowledge to dispose of her body at the building site. He looked like a strong suspect.

There was something else that Kelly had been considering and it was possible that Faye might be able to throw some light on it. "At Henderson's," she questioned, "do you ever hear of videos doing the rounds?"

"Videos?"

"Yes," Kelly responded. "Nothing too nasty. Just cheap stuff. Hauntings and horror."

"Well," Faye said, "you do hear of all sorts going round the men."

"Do you know where they come from? The videos, that is."

"Come away, darling," Faye said to James. "Evan's trying to watch that. Yes, good boy." Addressing Kelly again, she answered, "It's . . . er . . . rumoured they're made not a million miles away from here."

Kelly tried to extract more from her. "Where exactly?"

Faye kept her gaze on her son as she spoke. "The bloke at the video factory. He's supposed to be behind them, according to the rumours."

"Interesting," Kelly responded. "I just wanted to

know what Mum might have heard on the grape-vine. Do you think she would've known that as well?"

Faye shrugged. "Well, I heard, so I guess she might have."

Kelly nodded slowly and exchanged a knowing glance with Evan. Warr could have been lying when he said that their mother hadn't pestered him. And if she knew that he'd made the videos, she could have told George McCormick in the restaurant. Then, after her disappearance, he might have gone looking for evidence against Warr. That could be how he got himself killed.

Later, when Faye and James had left, Kelly managed to prise her brother's attention away from the football results. "I've been thinking," she told him. "Mum was in The Seafood Spree with McCormick. We have the manager's word on that. As we don't think he killed her, she was safe then. Yes? At some point that evening, though, she got into the hands of the killer. Right? But how?"

"What are you getting at?"

"When and where did she leave McCormick? From that moment she was vulnerable to attack. So, when did she stop being with McCormick and become a victim of . . . whoever?"

"How should I know?" Evan wasn't in the best of moods. He really wanted to watch the football results and not act as the great detective's sounding board. Yet the television coverage only reminded him that he was missing out on the real excitement at Revolvers. Often, when a result was announced, he thought to himself, I could have predicted that. I'd have been twenty quid up by now. His fingernails were taking extra punishment as his system reacted to emptiness.

Kelly continued her reasoning. "Mum was a woman. I doubt if McCormick would just let her make her own way home – or wherever she was going. He'd give her a lift. But if she was coming home . . ."

Evan showed some interest by mumbling, "Yes?"

"Well, he wouldn't give her a lift to the front door, would he? They might have been seen by Dad. So, he'd have dropped her round the corner or something."

"Yeah. Possibly. That's if she *was* coming home."

"I know. Let's assume that she was for now. The police asked everyone around here if they'd seen anything. No one reported a struggle on the street or someone yelling for help, so, if she was picked up by the killer near here, she didn't create a stir in the process."

Evan looked away from the TV screen for longer this time. "You're saying she was whisked away by someone she knew. Or she came home and Dad . . ."

"Let's not think about what Dad might have done. I can't imagine . . ." She shook her head. "No. But if your Pete had tried to drag her away, surely she'd have created a fuss. Someone would have noticed something. She'd seen Warr before, though. He might have enticed her into his car without her raising the alarm. And . . ."

"And?"

"Recently, I've been thinking about Vicky McCormick."

"I doubt if Mum knew her."

"No," Kelly agreed. "But two women are less likely to fight on the street. Mum wouldn't have been so wary of another woman."

"And Mrs McCormick could have played the police officer, anyway," Evan suggested. "Got out of an unmarked car, flashed her identity card, and asked Mum to get into the car with her. 'I'm afraid your husband's been in an accident, Mrs Keating. Please come with me. I'll take you to him.' That sort of thing."

"Yes! You're a genius, Evan, when you put your mind to it. She might even have been driving the family Peugeot. That would tie in with what we know. You might have got it."

"And," he added scornfully, "we might be barking up the wrong tree altogether. Perhaps she wasn't on her way home at all." He turned back to the television to watch some more sports news.

Wandering out of the room, Kelly murmured to herself, "Maybe. I have a hunch, though. I'm certain Vicky McCormick could make murder look like suicide. But," she wondered, "how do you investigate a police officer?"

Yet it wasn't just Vicky McCormick. Kelly's chief suspects still included Trevor Warr and Pete the bookie. All three of them had a connection with the building site and she could easily envisage a different motive for each of them. It surprised her how many people might have wanted to be rid of her mother. Was she such an ogre? To Kelly, she was just a normal mother who'd got bored with her life and her marriage. Taking on a job and a local businessman over planning permission had apparently not been enough to spice up her life – she'd needed a lover to do that.

The Keatings' situation had hardly been novel. Several of Kelly's friends at school were trying to cope with broken families. She'd been one of the few, though, with a mother who'd strayed; mothers were usually the devoted victims of wayward fathers. Now Kelly was unique amongst her friends; she was the only daughter of a murder victim. Even worse, she had inherited enough of her mum's obstinacy to want to solve the crime.

When Sarah returned, her boyfriend Matt was with her. He was a big lad with cropped hair, polite but uncomfortable in Mr Keating's presence.

Despite being brash and outgoing, he had not yet disgraced himself in front of Sarah's father so Mr Keating tolerated him.

As soon as he sat down Matt struck up a conversation with Evan as if he were under instructions to do so. "Are you still practising ball skills?" he asked.

Evan shrugged in reply.

"The Scorpions could do with more of that."

"Oh?" Evan responded. "Is the team in trouble?"

"No. Fifth in the league. Not bad. We can keep goals out but we can't score. That's the problem. We were wondering if—"

"No," Evan put in quickly. "I'd rather not."

"Okay." Matt's tone suggested that he'd kept his side of a deal but wasn't too upset by failure. He glanced at Sarah and shrugged.

Keen to follow up her new evidence, Kelly asked her sister how much she'd told Matt about the deaths.

"I don't keep any secrets from him," Sarah told her, patting Matt on the leg. "He might as well know what he's mixed up in."

Now that she felt free to talk in Matt's presence, Kelly outlined her conversation with Faye. Then she tried to get her brother and sister to agree on a way forward. "First," she proposed, "we've got to chase up our number one suspect."

"Who's that?" Sarah queried.

"Who do *you* think?" Kelly replied.

"Warr," she answered without hesitating.

"Mmm. Maybe. But I'm beginning to wonder about Vicky McCormick. What do you think, Evan?"

Evan pondered on it for a moment, then said, "I'll go with McCormick."

"Why?" Sarah retorted. Clearly she'd expected Evan to support her own choice. "You said you thought Warr had done it."

"Well, if you must know the truth," Evan muttered, staring at his own feet, "I'd just rather it wasn't Pete or Mr Warr. If either of them killed Mum, it'd be my fault. It was because of me that Mum might have tangled with them."

Both sisters looked sympathetically at him but he didn't see their concern.

"Okay," Kelly said. "I can understand that."

"But we can *do* something about Warr. We could take a look at the factory for clues or try and find this woman he said he was seeing that Thursday night. See if she backs up his story. Vicky McCormick's a real problem," Sarah objected. "We don't know anything about her. Where does she live? I bet police officers don't put themselves in the phone book. How do we get to her without going to the police?"

"You're right," Kelly answered. "We don't know anything about her, but it's not such a problem because we can find out about *Mr* McCormick instead. I imagine Faye can put her finger on his telephone number and address. They'll be on file at Henderson's. Then we can go and talk to her; exchange sympathies now we have a bereavement in common; see how she reacts."

"Maybe," Sarah mused. "But I still think Warr's more . . . you know."

"If I can make a suggestion," Matt put in, "you don't have to just go after your number one. There are four of us and three suspects. We could split up. Sarah and me, we could check out Warr's alibi. You could hunt down this policewoman, and Evan could follow up the bookie."

"Well, I'm not sure about Evan going after Pete," Sarah remarked, alarmed by the suggestion.

"Hang on," Kelly pronounced. "He might have a point. It doesn't have to be dangerous. Look," she said, "you don't have to go after Pete himself, Evan. You've just got to mix with your mates and find out if any of them saw Pete a week last Thursday. If so, when and where. We can rule him out if he was doing business that night. Can you do that? Can you do it without getting tangled up in more gambling? I don't want you to do it if you're going to get hooked again."

"No, I'll do it," Evan agreed. "And I won't get involved again."

Kelly smiled at her brother. She believed him.

"And you two," she said to Matt and Sarah, "you don't have to do anything risky either. In fact, I suggest you go out for a meal tonight instead of following Warr around. Maybe even three meals."

"What are you on about, Kelly?" her sister probed.

"Remember, Warr said he went for a Chinese that Thursday. I think there are three Chinese restaurants in town. He's bound to have reserved a table for two. He's that type. Wouldn't turn up on spec. So all you've got to do is to see their booking lists for that night. Go into all the restaurants, try to make a booking, and sneak a look at the list."

"All right," Sarah agreed, glancing at Matt. "We'll give it a go."

"That only leaves you," Evan said to Kelly in a rare display of concern for one of his sisters. "Seeing Vicky McCormick could be dangerous if . . ."

"Yes, but I'll make sure I tell her straight away that you three know all about my visit. Then she can't do anything to me, because you'd go to the police immediately."

The four of them accepted their tasks and, with a renewed sense of excitement and trepidation, went their separate ways.

Kelly persuaded Faye to sneak into work that same evening to look up the McCormick's address. Once she knew where the policewoman lived, Kelly decided to pay her a visit straight away. She was eager to get it over with.

She expected the house to be elaborate. It wasn't. It was one of a terrace of big, old and untidy houses – ideal homes for those with time to dedicate to their upkeep. Evidently the McCormicks did not have much spare time.

At the front door, Vicky was taken aback. She hesitated, then said, "You're the Keating girl. Kelly."

"Yes. Can I have a talk with you?"

Vicky glanced up and down the street before she replied. "Er . . . I suppose so. Come on in." She stood to one side to allow her guest to enter the dingy hall that ran the length of the house. She guided Kelly into the front room – a lounge containing bookshelves, a midi hi-fi system, a huge pile of cassette tapes, a couple of desks and a computer. Presumably, this was the machine on which McCormick's killer had left the note. There was also a photograph of the McCormicks standing together by a lake in happier times.

The police officer wasn't dressed in black but there was an air of sadness about her. Now that she was on her own, the big old house must have seemed eerie and forsaken. She cut a forlorn figure but, Kelly wondered, was her sorrow faked?

Vicky inquired how Kelly had found out her

address, then she asked, "Why have you come?"

"I spoke to Evan and Sarah about it. We thought I should. Because of . . . your husband and my mum. We have something in common now, don't we?"

"Apparently so," Vicky replied guardedly.

They sat opposite each other and looked blankly at one another for a few seconds.

"I need to know who I'm speaking to," Kelly began hesitantly. "Sergeant McCormick the police officer or Vicky McCormick the wife and ordinary person."

"Which would you rather talk to?"

"The wife of George McCormick."

"Well," Vicky said with a weak and wry smile, "I *am* on leave for a few days yet. Besides, if you want to talk about your mum and George, you can. It's a closed matter as far as we're concerned. My superior has tidied it up."

"Okay," Kelly replied. "I'm sorry about your husband. It's awful. But . . . do you believe Mr Tatton's version of events?"

Vicky stood up and turned away, lost in thought. When she looked again at Kelly, her eyes were red. In a fragile voice, she said, "I'll put the kettle on. Fancy a coffee?"

"Okay. Please."

While Vicky was out of the room, curiosity drove Kelly to examine the stack of cassettes. Each box was labelled with its contents – classical music – and the spine of each case bore the date of recording. They were organized in chronological order. She noted that the most recent tape bore the index, "St Petersburg Philharmonic: Sibelius Violin Concerto in D minor; Rachmaninov Symphonic Dances. BBC Radio 3." It bore the date of Thursday before last. An idea formed in her mind and she scanned back through the pile of tapes recorded last year. Eventually, she spotted what she wanted. It was there! One cassette had been logged on the thirteenth of October. "Ulster Orchestra: Schubert Symphony No. 5; Mozart Piano Concerto No. 12 in A; Schubert Symphony No. 6."

"George's collection," Vicky explained as she came back into the room with a couple of steaming mugs. "Not my thing, but he was mad on classical music. If he'd been here now the room would be throbbing with Beethoven or something." She looked haggard as she spoke. She probably loathed his obsession when he was alive and now lamented its absence.

Before taking the mug, Kelly stole a glance at the cassette recorder. It was a simple model and did not seem to have a facility for automatic recording at a pre-set time. Joining Vicky in the centre of the room, she clasped the mug. "Smells good," she said. "Thanks." She sat down again.

Vicky sipped her coffee and murmured, "Do I

agree with the DCI's conclusion?" Gazing straight at her guest, she answered, "I don't have a reason not to. Like you, I'm sorry as well. Sorry about your mum. And as far as George was concerned, we still loved each other, you know, but we tended to lead separate lives. I regret that now. I didn't know he'd taken up with your mum, but it didn't come as much of a shock. It's no great surprise to me that he got mad when she rejected him, either. He was like that, I'm afraid. Now it's all over, I'm just trying to forget it. I've got to get on with my life; there's not much else I can do. Wipe the slate clean and start again. I don't want to see it raked over."

Kelly thought she detected a hint of threat in Vicky's voice, but she wasn't sure. "I just thought it might help us both to come to terms with it if we had a chat," she said.

Vicky looked piercingly at her guest. "Is that all?" Steeling herself, she added, "You don't believe that George killed your mother and then himself."

It wasn't obvious to Kelly whether Vicky had made a statement or asked a question. In reply, she said, "You can't help wondering."

"Wondering what?" Vicky leaned forward. "It's all right; the case won't be reopened. You can say what you like."

Kelly took a gulp of coffee. Sooner or later she had to come to the point. She couldn't spend the afternoon skirting uselessly around it. "What if Mum *didn't* reject him?"

Without noticing it, Vicky slipped into her role of police officer. "You think someone else killed your mum?"

"And then maybe your husband."

Vicky shook her head. "What's your evidence?"

"We haven't got any. It's just . . ."

"Speculation?" Vicky suggested.

"Yes," Kelly agreed. Plucking up courage, she asked, "How did he die?"

"Drug overdose. He'd been on sleeping pills for some months. He took the lot."

"So, someone could have forced him to swallow them. The suicide could have been faked. Yes?"

"I can't disprove that," Vicky admitted. She shuffled in her seat and then continued, "It'd take some proving, though."

"When did he . . . er . . . you know?"

"He died at nine thirty. Pathology could be reasonably precise," she reported. "Besides, the time of his suicide note was recorded automatically by the computer. It was entered at five past nine." She let out a long weary sigh. "It's the police officer in me talking again. I want to forget the whole episode but . . . it rubs off on you, police work. It's not a job, it's a way of thinking. And it doesn't leave a lot of time for family life. Criminals don't keep a nine-to-five schedule, I'm afraid. Callouts round the clock. Not ideal for family life and certainly not for having children. He'd have loved kids, but . . . Don't get a job in the police force, Kelly. It's not worth it."

If Vicky McCormick was an actress, she was a good one. But Kelly already knew that. If she'd committed two murders, her performance during the investigation was brilliant. It would have to be. Any murderer who wasn't a good actor simply got caught.

Kelly wound up the visit as soon as she could. She thought she wasn't going to learn any more from Vicky, and besides, she was keen to follow up the two solid facts that she had learned.

Matt was in his element. He strode into The Jade Garden with Sarah in his wake, with all the assurance of a man with an American Express Gold Card.

"Table for two," he told the receptionist. "Booked earlier. The name's Jones. Vincent Jones."

The little man on the desk ran his finger twice down the booking list, mumbling to himself, "Mr Jones." Eventually, he looked up apologetically. "I'm sorry, sir. Did you make the reservation today?"

Matt gave a groan. "Yesterday. I called yesterday to reserve a table for tonight. In the name of Jones."

The receptionist flicked the pages, clearly at a loss. "I'm sorry, sir," he repeated. "There seems to be some sort of mistake."

"Look," Sarah put in nervously. "I'm sorry about this, but can you show me to the ladies' room while you sort it out?"

"Certainly," the man said, eager to prove that there was something he could do correctly.

As soon as the receptionist turned his back, Matt delved into the pages of the book of reservations. A week ago on Thursday – there it was. A reservation for two, listed as Mr and Mrs Warr, nine thirty. There was a tick beside the name. Matt took it to mean that the couple had turned up for their meal.

Returning to Matt, the receptionist said to him, "Sir, I've checked with the manager and I think we can accommodate you – to make up for our error. If you could just wait here a moment."

Scanning the menu, Matt took fright. The prices were out of his league. When Sarah returned he nodded to indicate that he had the information they needed. He also indicated the price of the meals. Sarah gulped. "Leave it to me," Matt said with a wicked glint in his eye.

When their host returned, Matt said to him, "It's a pity about this booking problem. I'd heard that The Mandarin was an excellent establishment."

The man gawped for a second, then replied indignantly, "Sir, this is The Jade Garden!"

"Oh! Sorry," Matt returned. "Wrong place."

The receptionist was still agape as Matt took Sarah's arm and led her swiftly out of the restaurant.

11

The Keatings got together with Matt after his match on Sunday afternoon, to compare notes. They knew that McCormick had died on the Thursday before last some time after nine o'clock. By car, the Chinese restaurant was probably fifteen minutes away from George McCormick's place. Trevor Warr could have left his studio at about eight thirty, driven to McCormick's house, committed a devious murder, then shot off to collect his young woman and arrive at The Jade Garden for nine thirty. It was possible, but not very likely.

Still keen not to dismiss her number one suspect, Sarah commented, "We don't know that he got to the restaurant on time. He could have been late. It may not have been such a rush."

"No," Kelly agreed. "But, as alibis go, it's not bad. That'd be a busy night by anyone's standards."

Evan had kept a low profile at Revolvers but had still managed to talk to a few of Pete's customers. One of the lads and a girl remembered doing business with him on the Thursday night of the murder. Both were uncertain about the time. "They're more worried about who's crossing the finishing line than checking the time," Evan explained. "One said he thought it was at least ten because he'd already had a few drinks at a club. But Laura – she's well addicted to it. She said she sold Pete her watch. It was a present from her dad, worth fifty quid at least. Pete gave her a fiver for it. The gambling bug gets you like that. And as soon as she's sold everything she's got, she'll start nicking things. She probably already has. Anyway," he declared, "she thinks the watch said twenty past nine when she handed it over. If that's right, Pete would never have got from McCormick's place to Revolvers that fast. So I reckon he's off the hit list."

"Yes," Kelly agreed. "If we can rely on this Laura."

"What about you, Kelly?" Sarah put in. "What's the verdict on Vicky McCormick?"

Kelly beamed like a messenger with good news. "Well, I found out some really useful stuff. The trouble is, I still don't know about the woman herself. She's either innocent or she's guilty and a cracking liar. Anyway," she continued, "McCormick died after an overdose of sleeping pills. If you believe police things on telly, it's hard to shoot or stab someone and make it look like suicide, but anyone could have stuffed him full of his own pills. The murderer could have looked in the bathroom cabinet or wherever and seen the bottles with his name on them. Ideal."

"The one who'd be bound to know where they were is his wife," Matt remarked.

"True," Kelly responded. "She didn't act like I imagine a murderer would, but I suppose murderers don't."

"As you said, she could be a cracking actress."

Kelly shrugged. "Anyway, I think I've got proof that he didn't commit suicide. Most nights, from seven thirty to nine, Radio 3 has a programme on classical music. Famous orchestras going through their paces. I looked it up in old newspapers. Thursday last week, George McCormick recorded it."

"So?"

"No one records a programme then kills themselves. Why bother with a tape if you're never going to hear anything again?" Kelly glanced at her audience and noted, with pleasure, their unspoken accord. "And that's not all. He had another cassette recorded on the thirteenth of October last year. That programme went out in the same slot as well.

I checked by phoning the BBC in London. Seven thirty to nine." Kelly stressed the time, then stopped talking to let the information sink in.

"But he was—"

"It doesn't mean anything," Evan objected. "He could have been miles away at the time. He could have used a timer switch."

Kelly grinned at her own foresight. "No," she retorted. "He didn't have one. I checked. It doesn't mean he was at home every minute from seven thirty till nine, but he must have been there at seven thirty."

"He was supposed to have left The Seafood Spree at seven thirty, according to Tatton," Sarah reminded them.

"Maybe he missed the first part of the concert," Evan suggested.

"Possibly," Kelly replied, "but I don't think so. The cassette started with Schubert's Symphony No. 5 and the BBC told me that was the first piece on the programme."

"This is ridiculous," Sarah put in. "We know he was in the seafood place."

"Maybe the owner – Perriman – didn't get the time right," Kelly suggested. "That's one explanation. But even if he was half an hour out, McCormick would still be pushed to bring Mum back – if he did – then drive home in time for the programme. There *is* another explanation, though."

"What's that?" Sarah queried.

"He wasn't in the restaurant."

"Hang on!" Sarah uttered. "The owner identified him."

"But his first description was a bit wide of the mark, if you remember what Tatton said. Perriman may have made a mistake. Maybe Mum was with someone who looks like George McCormick."

Trying to lighten the mood a bit, Matt said, "That probably rules out Vicky McCormick."

Kelly ignored the humour. "I saw a photo of him with his wife in his house. He looked tall. Judging by her height, I'd say he was six foot or thereabouts. With very dark hair. Almost black."

"That's what I told the police," Evan mentioned. "It certainly rules out Pete. And Mr Warr. He's too short and hasn't got enough hair. I haven't seen anyone who looks like McCormick."

"Henderson's got that beard, so he's not our man," Sarah commented.

"I don't know," Evan returned. "A beard isn't a permanent fixture. He may not have had it last October."

"He did," Kelly confirmed. "I remember Mum used to joke about the boss's big beard."

"What about your dad? He's nearly six foot, I should think, and he's got black hair," Matt observed.

None of the Keatings replied immediately. It

seemed too preposterous. Eventually, Kelly said, "No. There's a resemblance, I grant you, but it couldn't be. He'd be in the shop at that time on a Friday. He said so. And he wouldn't lie about taking his own wife out for a meal. Why should he?"

"Only trying to help," Matt rejoined.

"The whole thing's a puzzle," Kelly concluded. "And we don't even know if the man she had a meal with is the one who killed her. It's just a guess."

The others sighed. There was almost too much to contemplate.

"No one said this detective stuff was easy!" Kelly remarked. She seemed to be enjoying the challenge.

That night, Kelly examined her list of suspects again. Dad and Evan still occupied the top slots. Even after her findings so far, she had no good reason to discount either of them, but she was convinced that Evan was innocent. He wouldn't be throwing himself into the investigation so whole-heartedly if he had something to hide. Next came Trevor Warr. He'd have to be fleet-footed to be a serious suspect now. Eric Henderson? He was the only one on the list not known to have clashed with her mum. She worked for him and she had one of his envelopes in her handbag when she was killed, but so what? Kelly couldn't imagine a motive. Vicky McCormick, police officer and Oscar winner? "Perhaps," Kelly mumbled to herself. "She was certainly keen to keep the case closed." Pete the bookie? According to Evan, he knew all about computers. He could have organized the fake suicide note on McCormick's computer. But lots of people worked with computers and Pete seemed to have an alibi for the night Mr McCormick died.

It struck Kelly for the first time that she had assumed that McCormick's and her mum's murders had been committed by the same person. Why? Because they were too closely linked to be separate issues. Too much of a coincidence. "It's a good assumption," she deduced. "At least, I think it is."

Glancing at the list of clues, she realized that she'd made some progress. She could explain the note on Dinner Date in the handbag. The topic of Evan's argument had finally come out into the open. But the Peugeot ... "Forget it," she mumbled. "Mum had been in a Peugeot shortly before she died. Doubt if it was Pete's or Mr Warr's. So, she'd been in McCormick's car. No great surprise. But if it was on the evening of the seafood meal, it would implicate Vicky McCormick. The trouble is, there's no way of telling. Then there's the green jumper. Same problem. Could be anyone's. She'd probably come into contact with Evan's that same morning." One way or another, all of her suspects were familiar with the building site. "Vicky McCormick would have known about it through her husband." It left the poor description of her mum's dinner companion. "Why on earth did Perriman make a mistake?" She shook her head in frustration.

Matt was right, of course. It was uncomfortable to have to admit it, and she had only her memory of a photograph to rely on, but her father *could* be mistaken for George McCormick in poor lighting by someone who knew neither of them well. "Which," Kelly reminded herself, "was exactly how Perriman had seen one of them." She couldn't imagine, though, why her dad should shut up shop early, take Mum out for a meal, and then deny that it had happened. It made no sense to her. Unless . . . unless he had some reason to distance himself from her that evening. The thought made her shudder so she tried to shut it out of her mind by changing direction.

If George McCormick hadn't been with Kelly's mother on Friday the thirteenth, the long gap between murders made more sense. Kelly fancied that McCormick would have undertaken quiet investigations into his lover's disappearance. They would have taken time if he'd got no information from her that day. He might not have known where to start. Rather like us, Kelly thought. She didn't even consider how they were going to avoid the same fate as McCormick if they ever did catch up with the villain.

She added what she now knew about the timing of both crimes to her list. It didn't cast any new light on the circumstances.

The facts were still swimming round her brain like tireless goldfish in a bowl when she went to bed.

12

After a hard day's work in his shop, Clive Keating liked to relax in front of the television. Not that he saw a great number of programmes. Some time after the news, his eyelids would droop and he would become increasingly drowsy until his mouth opened and his head lolled. When Barbara Keating had been in the house, she'd often gone unnoticed in the evenings as well. This Monday's batch of repeats was enough to send a hyperactive child off to sleep, but even so, he wasn't snoozing. The television was on but he was simply lost in thought, his gaze fixed on the coffee table to the side.

The police had returned his wife's property. Her dishevelled handbag now sat on the table like a sad, unwanted relic and he stared at it from a distance, tears blurring his eyes.

Evan had been given the task of quizzing his dad about his movements on the night McCormick had been murdered. He wasn't looking forward to it. Now, surveying the scene in the living room, he was put off altogether. Something told him it wasn't the time to tease information from his dad.

"Oh," he muttered. "Mum's handbag."

His dad sniffed and replied, "I didn't want it, but they didn't give me a choice. They shoved it straight into my hands. Your mum's stuff." He exhaled loudly.

"Shall I take care of it?" Evan volunteered.

Mr Keating looked up at his son and nodded. "Yes," he answered. "You put it with the rest of her things."

For the last six months, Clive Keating had acted as if his wife were simply on an extended holiday. He'd not thrown out any of her belongings. He'd occupied only half of his own bedroom. It seemed that he had expected her back any day. Or perhaps he'd wanted to give that impression. None of his children had believed that one day she'd walk through the door and carry on as if nothing had happened. But maybe it had been too painful or too incriminating for their father to excise her from his life.

He shook his head then added, "There's something else. They said they can release the body now they've finished all the paperwork."

"The body? What are we supposed to do. . . ?" Evan stopped himself as he realized that he was about to ask a stupid question.

His father answered him anyway. "Give her a proper funeral."

"Yes," Evan responded. "Of course."

When Evan prised open the handbag in his bedroom, a small cloud of white dust blew into the air. It was like exposing an ancient tomb. Inside, the artefacts were all individually wrapped in plastic wallets. Presumably the police had sealed them like that and hadn't bothered to take them out again before returning the handbag.

Evan set about removing the articles one by one and extracting them from their packaging: a purse containing a modest amount of money, a couple of credit cards and her driving licence; various items of make-up; the infamous betting slip; a ring with a key to the house, a car key and another small key; a wad of tissues; a comb and a Biro; the envelope that Tatton had already queried, its postmark so smudged that Evan couldn't even tell where it had come from; a small mirror and an emery nail file. Nothing remarkable.

His bed littered with his mum's meagre possessions, he suddenly felt depressed. He never wanted to see her corrupt body again, so sitting among her things was the closest he'd ever get to her now. He felt hollow. He didn't blame himself entirely for the fact that she was dissatisfied with her humdrum life but, just by being her son, he had contributed to the millstone around her neck. Ironically, when he'd added excitement to her life by getting involved with crooks, that life had been cut short. If the dead still had desires, she'd probably now prefer the role of bored wife and mother.

He raked through the contents of her handbag again, hoping she had left a clue, but the only hopeful item was the keyring. What did the small key unlock? Evan didn't know.

After proving his expertise at the Chinese restaurant, Matt had taken Sarah to The Seafood Spree to try his luck with a photograph of her father. It was the most recent picture they could find, and showed him and his wife together.

Sarah hadn't dared to go into the seafood restaurant after Mr Perriman's display of impatience last time. Thinking that Matt would stand a better chance of success on his own, she'd lingered outside and waited for him to do the business. He wasn't exactly booted out into the street, but he didn't get a very warm reception. Mr Perriman had glanced suspiciously at the photograph of the Keatings, recognized Sarah's mum, denied ever seeing her dad, then ordered Matt to leave. As they'd walked away, Sarah had peeped over her shoulder to see him standing in the window of his restaurant scowling at them.

Kelly had visited Faye in an attempt to squeeze yet more facts out of her. Despite her prompting, Faye couldn't remember hearing any rumours that Eric Henderson and Barbara Keating had had disagreements. Kelly had also asked if George McCormick had behaved differently during the period between the discovery of her mother's body and his "suicide". Faye hadn't noticed anything particularly strange. "He came into the office a few times – maybe more than normal – and took away papers and computer disks," she'd reported, "but there's not much new in that."

Back at home, as soon as Evan showed Kelly the small key, she identified it. "It's either her jewellery box or vanity case. Or maybe her brief-case." Excitedly, she added, "You don't think she hid something in it, do you? Something that'll tell us what happened?"

Sarah shrugged but Matt answered, "No. That'd be too easy."

"Only one way to find out," Kelly murmured. "I suggest you go downstairs, Sarah, and keep Dad occupied. Evan and I can slip into their bedroom and try it out."

"All right," Sarah replied, both pleased and disappointed to be left out of the real action.

Kelly and Evan tiptoed into their parents'

bedroom. It reminded Kelly of jaunts on Christmas Eves of years ago when, as an over-excited and naughty girl, she would sneak downstairs to take a premature peek at her presents under the tree. In their mother's half of the bedroom, it also seemed appropriate to whisper and make hardly a sound. Respect demanded it.

"Here's the briefcase," Kelly breathed. She was about to extract it from the gap between her mum's wardrobe and her unused bedside cabinet when she groaned and left it to gather yet more dust. "No key'll fit that," she said. "It's got a combination lock. Let's try her vanity case. Over here. See, it *has* got a lock."

Evan tried the key but it didn't fit. "That's not it," he said in a hushed voice.

"Oh," Kelly murmured in disappointment. Treading softly towards the dressing table that had remained undisturbed for six months, she murmured, "Try this." The jewellery box had a layer of dust on it. "I think it's a safe bet that no one else has checked it out," Kelly muttered as she blew across the lid, producing a small puff of dirt. She handed the box over to Evan and pointed to the brass clasp.

"If there's a clue in here," Evan whispered, "it must be small." The key slotted into the lock and, after a couple of attempts, it turned and the clasp sprang upwards. Evan smiled and gave the box back to Kelly. It didn't seem right for him to forage in his mother's jewellery.

In silence, Kelly emptied the box, item by item, on to the dressing table. Familiar earrings and brooches tumbled out. There were two lockets. One contained a tiny photo of their dad, the other bore a picture of George McCormick. "No wonder she kept this under lock and key," Kelly commented softly.

"Yes. Let's hope Dad didn't see it. If he did, he'd have good reason to . . . Well, let's hope he didn't."

Kelly took the locket in her palm and examined it closely. On the back, it was engraved. Her eyes widened as she read, "Happy birthday. Love, G.M."

"Her birthday was the tenth of October so he must have given it to her just before she died," Evan mumbled. "You don't think Dad spotted it, do you?"

"No idea," Kelly answered. "But perhaps she *has* left us a clue." She looked dejected as she said it. Unwillingly, she was trying to come to terms with the fact that her own father had become a serious suspect.

They cleared up noiselessly, replacing everything in the jewellery box, locked it again and left the room as quickly as they could.

"Hey, Dad," Kelly said, bringing her father back

from the edge of sleep on Tuesday evening. "Made a mug of tea for you."

"Oh," her dad murmured. He wiped his eyes, sighed and, a little more awake, took the mug. "Thanks. Thanks very much. Do you want to borrow the car again?"

Kelly laughed. "No. I was in the kitchen feeling thirsty and made one for you as well." Actually, she had also been sifting through the television pages of the stack of old newspapers tucked away in a corner of the pantry. "There's something you can do for me, though," she added. "Cast your mind back to Thursday, a couple of weeks ago. You know, the night before we had that last visit from Inspector Tatton."

"Yes?" he queried, glancing at her suspiciously.

"Well, one of the girls at school videoed the new Bond film that night. She's invited me round to see it. Says it's great. But I'm not that bothered, unless it's really good. It started at nine, ITV, so you'd have got back in time for it – or at least only missed a few minutes. Knowing you, a sucker for that sort of thing, I bet you watched it. Was it any good?"

Her dad thought for a moment. "Thursday, you say?" He took a sip of tea, then said, "Yes, you're right, it was on. But . . . er . . . you should know what I'm like in front of the telly. It can't have been that good. I must have drifted off because I don't remember it."

"Not even a bit?"

He shrugged. "Bond jetting all around the globe, trying to stop a power-mad baddie. I think he was a drug dealer in that film. Lots of stunts. A chase with petrol tankers near the end."

Kelly smiled. "Sounds like a familiar plot. Perhaps I won't bother." She concentrated on her own drink of tea but she was thinking about her dad's reply. His description was vague enough to fit almost any Bond film. Perhaps he hadn't seen much of it at all. The only part he remembered distinctly was towards the end. That would be well after the time of McCormick's death.

Kelly was beginning to worry about her father. Had Mum's antics hurt him so much that he'd turned into a murderer? She hoped not. If she found proof of his guilt, she'd have to face a terrible dilemma. Should she keep quiet and let him get away with his crime of passion because he'd suffered enough? Or should she turn in her own father? She didn't want to have to make that decision. Yet she had worked out a method for checking her dad's movements that Thursday night. It would have to wait till this Thursday evening, though. She thought that she could persuade Sarah and Matt to take on the task, and she hoped they'd be able to clear his name.

*　　*　　*

The telephone rang on Wednesday, before Clive Keating got home. Kelly answered it – she was alone in the house.

"Is that one of the Keating girls?"

"Yes, Kelly," she replied, her face crinkling into a frown.

"Kelly," the caller repeated. "Good."

Her ear froze to the phone as she listened. She had never had a threatening call before and its impact was like a sudden right hook to the head.

"Stop messing in things you don't understand," the muffled male voice whispered.

It was like receiving a call from a dim and distant world. Yet the whisper into her ear somehow made the caller seem alarmingly close. "Who is this?" she stammered.

"Never you mind. Just listen. It's over. You can't bring back your mum or McCormick, so let it be."

The more she heard and the more the horror of the situation was displaced by curiosity and reason, the more she realized that she could be listening to a woman. If so, the female caller was using a voice as low-pitched as possible to make herself sound like a man.

"No more prying. You don't want to end up—"

The voice broke off from its threat. Kelly could just make out footsteps in the background. She could tell that the person on the phone was still on the line but he or she was waiting. There was the characteristic sound of a door opening then closing with a crash. It could have been a shop door, Kelly thought with a sinking feeling. A newsagent's door. Desperately, she tried to find alternatives. It could have been a restaurant door, the door at a builder's yard or even at a police station.

The unearthly voice started again. "You don't want to end up like your mum."

Her face pale, Kelly swallowed.

"They'll be pouring concrete into the bridge over the canal soon. If you carry on sticking your nose in where it's not wanted, you'll end up propping up the road. Understand?"

"Yes," she mumbled.

"Good. Just do what I say. Back off."

The phone went dead.

Quaking, Kelly flopped into a chair. She closed her eyes and breathed deeply for a minute. The telephone call had shocked her but, once she'd recovered, it made her more determined. It could even be considered a good sign. She must be getting close to the killer. Obviously she'd have to be careful from now on, but she hadn't been put off the investigation. In fact, she had learned something. The caller knew all about another building site and, in following one of their recent leads, they were barking up the right tree. Although Eric Henderson would know the building site best, they hadn't hassled him at all. He could be in the clear.

Much more likely was Vicky McCormick or . . . But would her own father threaten her like that?

Kelly was pleased to have spared Sarah the phone call. It would have scared her sister silly. If Sarah had taken it, the investigation would have been abandoned by now. Kelly decided not to tell anyone about it. It was a risk, she realized, to keep it to herself, but it was difficult enough to track down a murderer without having to do it on her own because the others had been frightened off.

Evan had put his mother's handbag away in one of her drawers but he'd thrown away the betting slip and left out the envelope. It was lying around in his bedroom, waiting to be taken downstairs and stored with the rest of the charity collection. He grabbed it and went down to the living room, then hesitated before he slipped it into the bag of stamps. Every stamp in the polythene bag had been torn from an envelope. The one in his hand was the exception, the only complete envelope. Why bother to bring home a whole envelope when only the top right-hand corner was wanted? It was a waste of space in her handbag. Evan glanced inside the envelope to make sure his mum hadn't concealed a clue there. It was definitely empty. Turning it over, he examined the back. Nothing had been written on it. No murderer's name scrawled in blood. The address of Henderson's Builders on the front looked correct and unexceptional. Along the edge on the left-hand side someone, probably his mum, had written in small figures, "0101". Evan stared at it for a while then shrugged. "What's that?" he mumbled to himself. "The start of a phone number?" He didn't know and he had no way of finding out. It's probably nothing, he thought. Even so, he didn't put the envelope in the bag; he took it back upstairs to his bedroom.

Most of the people on Clive Keating's newspaper round came into the shop to pay their bills but a few, mainly the old folk, found it difficult to leave their houses. For these customers, Clive collected their newspaper money each Thursday evening. It would take an hour, from eight to nine o'clock normally. He was always thankful for volunteers to do the collection but would not let Evan or the girls do it on their own on dark nights. This Thursday, though, Sarah offered to take on the chore with Matt as bodyguard and her father accepted gratefully.

At one house, an old lady answered Sarah's knock and came to the door with the correct money already in her bony hand.

"Thanks, Mrs Hegarty," Sarah said as she took the cash and filled in the small receipt. "Dad was going to come," she said, "but he's busy. He can't always do it himself like he did last week. Kelly came round the week before, if I remember." She looked at the woman to see how she reacted.

Mrs Hegarty shook her head. "I don't think so, dear. It was Mr Keating who called two weeks ago, I'm sure. He's a good man, your pa. Always has time for a few words."

"I must have got it wrong," Sarah replied. "When did he call?"

"Oh, I never take notice of time. It doesn't do to watch clocks at my age. It's always about this time, though."

In the next street, Mr and Mrs Sweeney were more helpful. After Mr Sweeney had answered the door, his wife called from the sitting room, "Who is it?"

Mr Sweeney bellowed into the house, "Mr Newsagent's daughter, after the money." His wife must have been deaf. He went to get some cash.

Once he'd paid, Sarah asked him, "When's the best time for us to collect the money?"

"Now, love, and not when your father does, that's for sure. I sits down to watch the news and . . . ding dong on the doorbell every Thursday. A right nuisance. When you does it you gets here just before nine. I reckon he natters too much on his way."

"More than likely. Did he come just after nine last week?"

"Yes. And the week before. And the week before that."

From inside, Mrs Sweeney bleated, "What's Mr Newsagent saying?"

"It's his daughter, Edie. She's . . . er . . . she's asking after your health." He grinned wickedly at Sarah. "It perks her up when people ask after her."

She returned his smile. "Well, thank you, Mr Sweeney. Thank you very much. We'll have to see what we can do about the timing in future."

Sarah hurried home with the news that her dad could be struck off the hit list. At the time of McCormick's murder, he was probably standing on Mr Sweeney's doorstep, keeping him from watching the start of the news.

"So," Kelly said, "Dad's out of it. That's a relief. And what's more, I think I can figure it out now." With her father off the hook, she could eliminate all of her chief suspects, apart from one.

"Oh?" Sarah responded. "Do tell us ordinary mortals."

"Well, like Dad, Pete the bookie and Mr Warr have both got alibis. Not perfect ones, but reasonable. Henderson's not a hot prospect—"

Evan interrupted. "Why not?" he demanded.

"No motive," Kelly answered. "And . . . That's it, really – no motive." She still didn't want to tell them about the phone call from the harassed killer.

"Leaving?" Sarah quizzed.

"Detective Sergeant Vicky McCormick," Kelly

announced. The policewoman with the deep voice, easily made to sound like a man's. "She's got the motive – and the Peugeot. She could've picked up Mum that night. On top of that, being in the police business, she wouldn't have much trouble faking her husband's suicide."

"What happened to the theory that it wasn't her husband in the restaurant with Mum?" Evan queried.

Kelly shrugged. "Perhaps Mr Perriman just made a mistake after all. He does see a lot of folk. It'd be easy to get confused."

Sarah and Evan gazed at their sister in silence. Eventually, Sarah said, "All right, but what do we do next?"

Kelly knew perfectly well what she was going to do next but, after the phone call, she didn't want to put anyone else at risk. "Not sure," she fibbed. "Let's think about it. It's Thursday now. We could tackle it at the weekend. Pool any ideas then. Okay?"

The others nodded their agreement.

But Kelly's mind was made up. She would confront Vicky McCormick. It would have to be somewhere public, to make sure she'd be safe. The policewoman could hardly do a repeat performance in front of a crowd. With a wry smile, Kelly thought of the ideal place. Tomorrow, Friday 13th April, she'd meet Vicky at The Seafood Spree. It might bring back Vicky's memory of that night six months ago.

Kelly reminded herself of Vicky McCormick's telephone number from Faye's notes, then checked that no one was within hearing range and picked up the phone. It rang six times before Vicky's throaty voice came on the line. "Yes?"

Taking a deep breath, Kelly inquired, "Is that Mrs McCormick?"

"Yes. Who is it?"

Kelly identified herself and continued, "I think we should meet again, don't you?"

"I've already told you what I think," Vicky replied, clearly irritated. "The last thing I want is to resurrect it all. Back off, Kelly."

Kelly listened carefully. The voice was different from yesterday's, but that was being muffled deliberately. It could easily have been the same person. The accent was much the same. And, if Kelly remembered correctly, yesterday's caller had also told her to back off. "I know," Kelly responded uneasily. "But I think I need to see you once more. That should do it."

"And are you after me myself, or me the police officer?"

"You."

Sergeant McCormick sighed. "I really think you should stop messing . . ." She paused, then added,

"But I expect your mind's made up."

"Yes."

Vicky relented. "Okay. It's your decision. When and where?"

Kelly arranged to meet her the next evening at six o'clock in The Seafood Spree.

Just one last thing to do. She dialled the restaurant and announced herself to Mr Perriman. At first he sounded peeved. "Don't worry," she reassured him, "I just want to come for a meal this time."

"Really?"

"Yes. Tomorrow at about six."

Mr Perriman sounded less harsh. "Well, I can certainly accommodate you at that time. You don't need to book a table. Just come along."

Kelly put down the phone, feeling relieved. Yet she told herself that the serious business was only just beginning.

13

Kelly hesitated as she made for The Seafood Spree after school in the early evening of Friday the thirteenth. She had a few misgivings, she was nervous, but she was also determined. She was fifteen minutes ahead of schedule yet she did not linger for long. She strode along the streets towards the restaurant.

It was six thirty when the doorbell rang insistently. Only Sarah and Evan were at home and Evan got to the door first. Sarah flew down the stairs in case Matt had arrived. She stood behind Evan and her jaw dropped as the door opened to reveal Kelly's number one suspect, Vicky McCormick. Neither Evan nor Sarah said anything. They just waited for the policewoman to explain herself.

"It's Kelly," Vicky started. "She arranged to meet me at six in The Seafood Spree but she didn't turn up. Is she here?"

"She was meeting you?" Sarah queried over her brother's shoulder.

"Yes. She arranged it last night, by phone. Can I come in?"

"Just a minute," Evan objected, still blocking her way in. "Why was she seeing you?"

"I'm not sure. Something about your mum and my husband, I imagine."

"And you say she didn't turn up?" Sarah checked. Like her brother, she was thinking that it would be very easy for Vicky McCormick to claim that she hadn't seen Kelly. The truth could be much more serious. She began to fiddle with the pendant round her neck.

"That's right. I went to the restaurant. I was a bit late and Kelly wasn't there."

"Perhaps she'd left," Evan suggested. "Didn't want to wait."

"That's what I thought but Mr Perriman – the manager – hadn't seen her either. If she set out for the restaurant, she didn't get there. I got worried about her. Thought she might be here."

"No," Evan answered. "She could've forgotten. Maybe she's at some party. She likes parties."

"Kelly doesn't forget things," Sarah commented.

"Then I *am* worried," Vicky said. "I think you'd

better come with me while I sort this out."

Evan glanced back at his sister. She was frowning. If this woman at the door had captured Kelly, she might be after both of them now. He turned to their visitor again and muttered, "This isn't official, is it?"

"You mean, is it police business?"

"The police always go around in twos. This isn't official."

"No," Vicky admitted. "But I think I'd better follow it up."

"Without us," Evan announced. He felt that the detective sergeant might be conning them. "If it's not proper business, you can't force us. We won't come."

Vicky McCormick looked surprised and disgruntled. She exhaled, then shrugged. "You're right, I can't force you. Not yet. But — never mind, I'll do it myself." As a parting shot, she said, "I think Kelly's been dabbling in things best left to the police. Let this be a warning to you. Don't you two start as well."

The off-duty police officer walked away and Evan closed the door. He was left looking at a pale, trembling sister.

"What do we do?" she uttered.

"First, we have a think," Evan replied. With Sarah in his wake, he slipped into the living room.

As soon as he sat down, he got up again. "*Yellow Pages*," he mumbled.

"What?" Sarah inquired.

"I'll call the fish place and check out Vicky McCormick's story."

"Good idea."

Mr Perriman came to the phone eventually and confirmed what the policewoman had stated. "Your sister," he complained. "She phoned to say she was coming and then she doesn't appear. It's not good enough."

Evan didn't answer the criticism. He simply said, "Thank you." He nodded at Sarah and told her, "She wasn't lying. Not about that anyway. Kelly didn't show up. But," he added, "maybe she didn't show because Vicky McCormick waylaid her."

Sarah was on the verge of panic. "Don't tell me Friday the thirteenth's repeating itself, this time *before* a meal at the seafood restaurant. We've got to do something. Kelly could be . . . I don't know. She could have been kidnapped on the way there."

"Yes," Evan agreed thoughtfully. "By Vicky McCormick, or . . ."

"Or who?"

"Or anybody."

"Like?"

"Any of our suspects. We've no idea where they are now and what they're up to. Not even Dad."

Sarah's mouth hung open. She was lost for words.

"But it's probably Vicky McCormick," Evan continued, partly to put Sarah out of her misery, and partly because his father wasn't his prime suspect.

"That's right," Sarah retorted at last. "We've ruled out most of the others, including Dad."

"One thing's for sure, though," Evan said. "It strikes me that we need to solve this right now. Kelly could be in trouble."

Sarah agreed. In the midst of her anxiety, one thing pleased her: Evan was speaking like one of the family. For the last few months he wouldn't have shown such brotherly concern. Now the Keatings were beginning to operate like a unit again. Yet she was scared. She feared that they were about to lose Kelly just as they had all started to pull together as a family should, especially one that had lost its mother.

"So," Evan continued, "it's time I was on my bike."

"What do you mean?"

"It won't take me long to pay a few visits on my bike. I'll call in at the shop and check out Dad. I reckon I know where Pete and Mr Warr will be, so I can take a sneaky look at them as well."

"Pity you can't pedal fast enough to chase Vicky McCormick in her car," Sarah commented. "That would be more useful."

"I'll leave that to you. You need the Matt Mobile. Why don't you give him a call? The two of you can drive to McCormick's place. Kelly wrote down the address – it'll be in her room somewhere. See if you can spot anything suspicious at the house."

"Like signs of Kelly?"

Her brother nodded. "Okay?" he asked.

"I suppose so. You be careful."

"And you," he replied as he headed for the garage.

His bike was doubly locked. It was shut inside the garage and its front wheel was anchored to the frame with a combination lock. Too many bikes disappeared from the district to take risks. Evan knelt down by the front wheel and dialled in the code to release the lock: 2511. It was easy to remember the number because it was his birthday: 25th November. Before he lined up the third digit, he dropped the lock and stood bolt upright. He remembered that it was his mother who had suggested the birthday code. And, Evan reasoned, if she'd suggested it for him, maybe she'd used the same system herself. That would be 1010 in her case. And upside down, it would look like 0101! Evan gave up on the idea of taking to his bike. Instead he flew back into the house.

In his bedroom, he grabbed Henderson's envelope

and turned it the other way up. It was there. Written down the side. 1010. His mother had left a clue after all.

"Sarah!" he yelled.

His sister bounded up the stairs as if his bedroom were on fire. "I thought you'd gone," she said when she saw that there wasn't an emergency.

"Nearly. But take a look at this first." He handed over the envelope and pointed to the hand-written number. "I think that's a message from Mum. And I bet it's the combination that opens her briefcase."

"Really?"

"Yes. Do you want to find out?"

Sarah looked unsure. She didn't like the idea of delving into her mum's things.

"If it is a clue, she wrote it because she wanted us to find it," Evan insisted. "She wouldn't have left the combination – if that's what it is – if she didn't want us to use it."

"No, I suppose not," Sarah replied. "All right, let's go and get it over with. For Kelly's sake."

In their father's bedroom, Evan dragged the dusty briefcase out of its niche. "It's not heavy," he said with some disappointment. "I hope there's something in it after all."

"She didn't use it much," Sarah commented. "Occasionally for work. Put a newspaper and sandwiches in it. That's about all."

Evan balanced the case on a bedside chair and thumbed the ratchet till he had dialled 1010 on the left-hand clasp. He pulled back the fastener and the lock sprang open. He glanced at Sarah and said, "Told you!" He lined up the same number on the right-hand catch and opened it. Hesitating before lifting up the lid, he muttered to his sister, "Keep your fingers crossed."

The briefcase wasn't quite empty. At the bottom there lay a single piece of A4 paper. It was a letter from a supplier of building materials and it was addressed to Mr E. Henderson of Henderson's Builders. Evan picked up the letter and held it up so that both he and Sarah could read it.

The first paragraph confirmed an order for hundreds of tonnes of aggregate at a discount cost.

"What's aggregate?" Sarah queried.

"I think it's added to cement to make concrete," Evan answered.

The second paragraph was much more interesting.

We are obliged to point out that this aggregate can be supplied at this low price because its quality restricts its use. It is excellent for concrete that does not bear stress. Concrete made with this material has medium compressive strength, as shown in the accompanying technical data, but, if it were to be used for load-bearing walls, its limited tensile strength would provide little resistance to impact. Such concrete failed controlled impact tests.

Evan and Sarah looked at each other. They realized that they had read something significant but the message was slow to sink in.

"What does it mean?" Sarah muttered.

"I'm not sure," Evan replied. "But . . ."

"Has it got anything to do with Mum? And Kelly?"

"I wonder if we've been ignoring the one real piece of evidence we've got," Evan said. "It's been staring us in the face and we've ignored it."

Sarah interrupted his thoughts. "What are you talking about?"

"Concrete evidence!" Evan declared. "Literally."

"You mean, why did the wall fall down?"

"Exactly," Evan cried, becoming more animated as he worked it out. "It's not normal for cars to knock down a concrete wall when they crash into it at no great speed, is it? The car should have come off worse. The wall was weak. It had lots of cracks. I don't know exactly what this letter means but it's definitely a warning not to use this aggregate stuff in important walls."

"You're saying Henderson used it anyway," Sarah deduced. "He was warned it wouldn't stand up to impact but he used it anyway."

"That's right. It was cheap so he used it. He was

cutting corners. It's almost like . . ." He paused, then continued, ". . . like Mum was trying to tell us something when she fell out of the concrete."

Sarah groaned and turned away, but soon looked back at her brother. "It was built badly. So what?"

"Not just badly, it's probably criminal. And Mum knew."

Sarah nodded slowly. She peered closely at the letter and commented, "This is a photocopy. She must have seen the letter at work one day. She knew the place was being built badly, so she copied the letter as proof and brought it home to keep it safe."

"Yes. She brought it home in her handbag, in the original envelope. That's why the envelope was still complete. She took the letter out, dumped it here and the envelope stayed in her handbag. Then she'd have gone to put pressure on her boss. Blackmail him. Threaten to tell someone about dodgy workmanship if he didn't drop the building." Evan paused only to get his breath. He continued, "She could have blackmailed Henderson to stop the work going ahead. And if Warr tried to get someone else to carry it on, she could have planned to threaten him with leaking information about the videos. She must have believed she could halt the building."

"Henderson . . ." Sarah mumbled. "Do you think he killed Mum to stop her talking?"

"It fits," Evan concluded.

"I must admit, it might explain something that's been bothering me. We've been guessing that George McCormick spent five months or so investigating her disappearance and getting nowhere. Then, a few days after the wall collapsed and Mum . . . you know, he got close enough to the killer to get himself killed. It was too much of a coincidence for him to sort it out just then. But he was in the building trade. He'd know that the wall shouldn't have collapsed. That was his big clue. He saw it, we didn't."

"Could be," Evan agreed. "He can't have found this evidence," he said, waving the letter, "but he might have challenged Henderson anyway, just because he knew that something was wrong with the wall."

Sarah was thinking back to the information that Kelly had gleaned from Faye on Monday. "Didn't Kelly say that Mr McCormick went to Faye after Mum's body was found and asked for lots of files and floppy disks? Perhaps he was looking for proof."

"Yes, I think she did. I doubt if he found anything. Perhaps he tackled Henderson anyway – out of frustration."

"Hang on," Sarah put in. "It still doesn't quite fit. Henderson wasn't with Mum in the seafood restaurant that night. She was with George

McCormick or someone who looks like him. I never saw George McCormick but, if he looked like Dad, Eric Henderson's nowhere near."

"That's true," Evan conceded. "Henderson's much shorter and tubbier, and he's got that great beard."

"There's something else. Why should Kelly disappear? She was after Vicky McCormick, not Henderson. If she wasn't threatening him, he wouldn't be out cruising the streets trying to grab her. It doesn't make sense."

"I see what you mean," Evan replied. "But . . . er . . . I wonder if it makes sense if Vicky McCormick's in on it as well."

Sarah's brain went into overdrive. "Now that's a real possibility. They both stood to gain. Henderson removes the threat to his livelihood by killing Mum and Vicky McCormick gets rid of an unfaithful husband – and his lover. Vicky could have called Henderson to tell him that Kelly was hounding her. Together, they'd want to get her off their backs. I think you've cracked it, Evan!"

"Yeah," Evan murmured, without enthusiasm. "It means Kelly's in deep trouble."

They both jumped and then ducked down below the level of the bedroom window as the doorbell suddenly chimed.

"Is that Vicky McCormick back again?" Sarah whispered urgently.

"How do I know?" Evan responded. Keeping low, he sneaked up to the window and carefully peered down on to the street. Then he let out a groan. He stood up, turned to Sarah and said, "The Matt Mobile's out there."

"Phew!" Sarah sighed. "Matt's arrived. Good. We need him."

"Well," Evan retorted, "we need his car at any rate."

At the front door, Matt chirped, "Sarah Keating? Your taxi's here." Then he saw her face. "What's up?" he said.

"It's Kelly," she began as she let him into the hall. "And we think we know who did it."

Once they'd updated Matt, he asked, "So where do you want to go?"

"McCormick's place, I should think," Sarah replied.

"There are alternatives," Evan declared. "Like Henderson's yard. Or . . ."

"Or what?"

"Let's assume that McCormick and Henderson have got Kelly," Evan reasoned. "If they've got a choice, they wouldn't take her to either of their houses or to the builders. It'd be too risky, in case they were seen with her. They'd take her somewhere else."

"Like?" Sarah encouraged him.

"It *is* Friday the thirteenth again."

Sarah and Matt glanced at each other and then they both stared at Evan. "You don't mean . . ."

"I mean, they could have taken her to a building site. Just like they did with Mum."

The full horror of Evan's words was still hitting Sarah as Matt said, "So where's Henderson building stuff these days?"

"Down by the canal," Evan suggested. "They're putting up a new bridge."

"What are we waiting for?" Matt responded. "Let's go."

14

From the back seat of the car, Evan pointed over Matt's shoulder. "Park there," he called. "We can walk down the towpath to the site. If anyone's about, they won't see us coming if we're careful."

It was seven thirty and the April evening was overcast. The gloom made it seem later. It wasn't cold but rain threatened. As they approached the ancient brick bridge that had come to the end of its useful life, they wished it was darker.

"The new bridge is going up on the other side of this one," Evan said as they lingered out of sight behind the old one. "Once we're out of its shadow, we'll be in the open. There's a fence round where they're building, but some of the kids at school come down here and mess around. They say you can get under it in one place on this side. We'll have to find the hole, and hope we're not spotted."

"Okay. Do you want to lead?" Matt asked Evan.

"All right. Follow me. Quietly."

"Do you want the torch?" Matt said, holding it out to him.

"No, you keep it. The last thing we want right now is to announce that we're here."

They stole out from the dinginess of the bridge, Evan first, and crept towards the wire fence. Beyond it, there was a steep slope up to a wide muddy track, that one day would be a proper road, leading to the edge of the canal. A big truck was parked on the embankment. Where the track stopped there was a wooden tower surrounded by steel scaffolding – a mould into which concrete would be poured to form a support for the new bridge. On the opposite side of the canal, the other support had already been erected. Once the second concrete pillar had been completed, the beam of the bridge would be lowered into place by the crane, which stood waiting like a giant guardian of the silent building site.

"No one's about," Sarah whispered.

"Good," Matt replied.

"But Kelly could still be here. She might be in this tower."

"She'd be yelling for help."

"Not if she's gagged," Evan speculated. "Or knocked out."

"Charming!" Sarah muttered.

"He's right, though," Matt said.

"Let's check out this fence," Evan suggested.

The three of them crouched down and inched their way along the perimeter, stopping sometimes to tug at the wire webbing to test its sturdiness. About fifty metres away from the towpath, Evan grabbed hold of the fence, yanked, and found himself flat on his back in the mud. He sat up quickly. "Here it is." The wire netting had come away in his hand. It wasn't a big hole, but it was enough to crawl through. Evan went first, then Sarah, and finally Matt slipped into the compound. They stood on the wrong side of the fence and their hearts beat faster. They had become trespassers.

"Up here," Evan breathed.

They scrambled up the bank and on to the mud track that ended suddenly with the tower at the edge of the canal. Feeling very exposed, they crept along the track, pausing by the lorry, where they were shielded from the housing estate on the other side of the mound.

"I'm sure we're being watched," Sarah muttered, imagining prying eyes everywhere.

"Think of Kelly," Matt said. "We haven't got a choice. It's not far to the end. Even if someone's watching, we can get her out – if she's there – and leave here in a few minutes."

There was a small gap between the end of the track and the wooden frame. It was bridged by a plank.

"You go on and check," Evan murmured to Matt. "You've got the torch. We'll keep watch in case anyone comes."

Before he put his whole weight on the plank, Matt tested its stability by pressing on it with his foot. It seemed perfectly safe so he walked its short length and peered over the wooden frame and down into the murky depths of the tower. He couldn't see to the bottom so he called into it, "Kelly?" He concentrated, trying to hear the faintest reply, but there was nothing, only the echo of his own voice coming out of the hollow. He switched on the torch and directed its beam into the cavity. It picked out the rough wooden sides, some steel rods that would reinforce the concrete and, at the bottom, gravel. There was no sign of a victim of abduction.

Over his shoulder, Matt cried softly, "She's not here."

Sarah and Evan looked at each other and shrugged.

"Just as well, really," Matt reported as he crossed the plank, "because I can't see how we'd have got her out of there."

Sarah was crestfallen. "What now?" she mumbled.

"We get out of here for a kick-off," Matt answered.

Evan led the way down the embankment, through the hole in the fence, and back on to the towpath. Standing underneath the old bridge, he said, "Of course, there are other places where bridges are being built. I don't know if it's Henderson's that's putting them up, though. She could've been taken to any one of them."

"You mean the new ring road?" Matt checked. "You're right. There's at least a couple of bridges going up for it."

"Back to the car, then," Evan concluded. "We'll have to take a look."

Sarah disliked the idea. She'd had enough. Yet she also knew that they had little option. She confined herself to a low moan and plodded after Evan.

For a short distance on the outskirts of town, the old road ran parallel to the new. The ring road itself was not far from completion but some bridges were still under construction. Matt stopped the car at a bus stop that was separated from the first building site by a small field. The sun had gone down but, by the spotlights of the works area, they could see that the great concrete columns and arch were almost finished.

"Not that one," Evan said without even getting out of the car. "Let's try the next."

Matt pulled away from the kerb. "The next one's about half a mile down the road, I think," he said. "There's a track for the lorries, cranes and the like to get to it."

"Fine," Evan replied. "We'll take it as well."

When he came to the track, Matt turned left, past the sign that read "Construction vehicles only". It was a bumpy driveway and he crawled along it in second gear despite wanting to put his foot down to get out of sight of the main road as quickly as possible.

The landscape was unreal. Motionless machinery lay everywhere, like petrified dinosaurs in a barren terrain. Heaps of sand and gravel stood on a half-made road that ended abruptly a few metres short of an artificial cliff – a chasm soon to be spanned by concrete. A fluorescent ribbon fluttered as a warning of the sheer drop. Here and there steel skeletons like playground climbing-frames poked out of the foundations, waiting to be enveloped in concrete to form unimaginable structures.

Matt brought the car to a halt and Evan got out and glanced around. It was like stepping out of a spacecraft to help in the construction of a lunar colony. But the crew that should have been there had vanished mysteriously, leaving tools scattered all around.

"Weird!" Sarah exclaimed.

Only the distant strings of street lamps and rows of house lights reminded them that they were not far from familiar territory.

"Well," Matt said. "Here we go again."

Side by side they walked towards the heart of the compound. Suddenly, they froze. Harsh spotlights had come on and blazed down unforgivingly on them as if they were footballers in a stadium at night. Instinctively, they all ducked down. "Over here," Evan whispered. He led the way and they crawled behind a dump truck, where they were shielded from the worst of the glare.

Leaning against one of the enormous tyres, Sarah muttered, "Someone's seen us."

"I'm not so sure," Matt responded. "I don't think anyone's here. It's more likely to be a security system: infrared detectors. They sense movement and turn on the main lights automatically. I think we've just got to carry on, ignore the lights, and hope for the best. Otherwise we might as well give up and go home right now. We'll have to hope no one can be bothered to report that the lights are on."

Evan shrugged. Making the best of it, he said, "At least we won't need a torch."

They got to their feet and, still uncomfortable in the dazzle, headed towards the first of two huge wooden structures. In a day or two, they would be filled with concrete and then stripped of their framework to reveal supports for the bridge, designed to be strong enough to take the weight of four lanes of traffic over the river below. Where the tarmac of the new dual carriageway stopped, compressed earth sloped gently up to the top of the temporary towers. Tomorrow, lorries would trundle up the ramp and pour concrete sludge into the cavities.

Taking a last look about them, Evan, Sarah and Matt put their hands on the top of the wooden wall and peered over. The security lights pierced most of the cavern below them, revealing a network of thick steel wires that would strengthen the concrete pillar. They cast ominous shadows on the inside surface of the frame, making it look like a cage.

"Can you see to the bottom?" Sarah asked.

"Just about," Matt replied.

"I don't think there's anything in here except these cables, but it's a long way down," Evan added.

"The torch won't help a great deal," Matt commented. "It's not powerful enough to make much of an impression down there."

Sarah called into the hole, "Kelly? Are you there?"

Nothing. It was as if she had shouted down a deserted mine shaft. The void swallowed her words.

"Let's try the next one."

They ran down the ramp, crossed on to what would become the second carriageway and hurried up the next slope.

Inside, the cavity was the same: hollow, eerie, and riddled with steel bars. It reminded Evan of a dreadful prison. Otherwise, it seemed empty. "Kelly!" he cried into it.

His lonely voice bounced back.

Sarah sighed, fighting to keep back tears of weariness and dismay. She couldn't bring herself to admit it aloud but she was wondering if Kelly was lying unconscious or even dead at the bottom of one of these grim holes. Her own sister, so full of life, condemned in one of these awful pits! Sarah wanted to run away but she wanted to stay too. She hated the building site but leaving it meant giving up.

"I'm not sure if there's another place like this further down the road," Matt said. "There might be. We could try—"

"Shush!" Evan snapped. "Listen. I heard something!"

They peered as far as they dared over the belly of the earth and concentrated in silence. It seemed like a minute but it was only a few seconds before Matt murmured, "Wishful thinking."

Frantic, Sarah called, "Kelly?"

At first, there was no answer. Then they heard it: a weak but definite clang.

"Yes!" Matt confirmed when they looked at each other. "There's something."

The metallic noise sounded again.

"It's Kelly!" Evan cried. "She's down there! I can't see anything; she must be in shadow. But she's banging on the cables."

Sarah wanted to roar with relief and scream with horror at the same time. Instead, she muttered, "What are we going to do? She must be in trouble. We've got to get her out."

"Give me the torch," Evan said to Matt.

"Why?" Matt asked.

"Why do you think?"

"You can't—"

"What are you two talking about?" Sarah put in.

Evan took off his coat, handed it to Matt and snatched the torch. "I'm going down," he said.

"But . . ." Sarah looked over the edge again. "How? It's not possible."

"These steel bars – they're like a ladder. I can use them to climb down."

"You can't be serious!" Matt spluttered. "You can't even reach one from here."

"I can," Evan replied. "I'm going to stand on the edge and you're going to steady me. From there I can jump and catch that nearest cable. The rest is easy." He slipped the torch into his trousers' pocket, ready for action.

"No!" Sarah yelled. "You'll get yourself killed. It's a long way down."

"Yes," Evan answered. "That's why I don't intend to miss that steel bar. Well, are you just going to stand there or are you going to steady me before I jump?"

"I can't help you kill yourself."

"Look, I'm a good climber. And if you've got a better idea to get Kelly out, I'll listen to it."

Neither Matt nor Sarah could reply.

"Right," Evan said. "While I'm down there, you try and find planks that'll stretch from here to the steel frame. I'll need them to get out when I come back up with Kelly. We haven't got the time to look for them now. I'd rather jump and get it over with. Help me up."

"I'll say one thing," Matt murmured as he gripped Evan's arm, "you've got guts enough for two."

"Just don't let me fall before I jump," Evan replied as he clambered up on to the edge of the frame. "And when you feel me take off, let go straight away. Whatever you do, don't hold me back."

Matt held Evan steady by his right arm and Sarah clasped one of his legs as he stood on high like a man on the gallows. She could feel his leg trembling – or maybe it was her own arm shaking.

Evan breathed deeply. "Get ready to let go," he

whispered without looking at them. Perched on the edge, his gaze was fixed on the steel skeleton. All his concentration was focused on one of the rods. He did not look down to see the great chasm between him and the steel bar.

He flexed at the knees and then threw himself forward with all his strength, like an Olympic swimmer diving into a pool. He leapt out over the void.

Sarah screamed.

Evan let out a cry as he hit the network of cables with a tremendous thud. His fingers closed round the first horizontal rod but, with the force of his collision and the sweat on his hands, they could not keep a grip and he slipped. With nothing below his legs he began to fall. Desperately, he clutched at the second bar. This time his fingers made contact and he got a hold. He shuddered to a halt, wrenching his arms, but maintained his grip so that he dangled alarmingly in mid-air. Flailing his legs till he found a firm foothold, he clung on to his make-shift ladder while his frenzied heart-beat slowed to merely wild. He fought for his breath as if he'd just completed a marathon.

"Are you okay?" Sarah called across the divide.

"Yeah," he answered without turning his head. "A good few bruises, but I'm okay. It's just like a climbing frame, only bigger. I'm going down. It shouldn't take long. You go and find a plank or two. I don't fancy being stranded here when I come back up."

"All right," Matt responded. "Good luck."

Evan began to descend into the pit. It was like going down an endless ladder but the rungs were further apart and not so regular. Sometimes he had to stretch with one of his legs to reach the next bar. When he stopped to relax his aching muscles, he yelled into the blackness below, "Hold on, Kelly, I'm coming." Out of the brightness of the flood-lights, it got darker and darker as he slowly made his way down. The air smelled stale and damp.

Eventually his foot, probing for the next rung, made contact with solid ground. It was the concrete foundation for the pillar, and the vertical rods that he'd used as a ladder were embedded in it. He took out the torch and flashed it around. "Kelly?" he called.

She was behind him and all she could do was moan. There was a handkerchief gagging her mouth and her wrists were tied by a short length of rope. Her trousers and jumper were stained and torn. She looked like a white-faced scarecrow.

Evan put down the torch so it illuminated her, knelt down and untied the gag first.

"Ugh!" She spat out the taste of the handker-chief.

"Are you okay?" Evan asked as he began to work on the rope.

Kelly was in no fit state to answer. She simply stammered, "I can't tell you what I felt when I saw the lights come on and heard your voice." She threw her freed left arm around her brother, hugged him tightly and cried without restraint.

Eventually she regained her composure, wiped her face and sniffed. She muttered into his ear, "Thanks."

"I guess it was Henderson," Evan said.

Kelly nodded. "He pushed me down."

"You fell all the way down here?" Evan was amazed.

"Yes."

"So how come you survived? It's some drop."

"I've got some bad news for you," she muttered. "I hit these wires on the way down. I couldn't keep hold with my hands tied, but I did enough to break the fall by grabbing a few cables."

"Wow. Sounds painful."

"Yeah. The trouble is, I can't move my right arm," she admitted. "I think it's broken. It hurt enough, but now it's just numb."

Evan groaned. "Can you stand?"

She held out her good arm as an invitation to be pulled to her feet.

Evan drew her up gently till she was standing shakily. "Well," he said, "that's a start. But you can't climb a difficult thing like this with one hand. It's not possible."

Kelly looked apologetic. "Sorry," she mumbled.

"It's not your fault," he replied. "But . . . er . . . we've got a problem. We can't wait for help to arrive. Henderson could turn up any moment with those security lights blazing away. We need to crack on. So, how are we going to get you back up?" He paused before continuing, "I know. You can't climb with one arm but you can have a piggyback. You can hold on to me with your good arm."

"What?"

"Look. I'll need to keep my arms free for climbing. They'll be up here." He demonstrated by holding both arms up in the air. "You can thread your left arm round my shoulders and cling on to my waist or something with your knees."

"You can't clamber all the way up there with my weight on your back!"

Evan looked up towards the light, turned to Kelly and shrugged. "Piece of cake," he lied. "But if you think your arm hurt before, by the time we get to the top, it'll be torture."

"I know." She tried to smile at him. "It won't be easy for you either. But I guess we haven't got much choice."

Evan turned his back and held his arms up. "Come on, let's get cracking. Just keep your bad arm sandwiched between your chest and my back. Keep it as still as you can. I'll try not to jolt about too much."

"Never mind me," Kelly replied, climbing awkwardly on board. "Just concentrate on getting up. I'll try not to groan too much in your ear."

Evan reached up for the first rod and stepped on to the lowest rung. It was then that the enormity of the task struck him. Kelly wasn't heavy but she wasn't light either. After a few metres she'd seem unbearable. She also restricted his movement so much that climbing wasn't going to be easy. "Okay?" he asked her.

"Yes," she said in a voice that ached to cry, No! I feel like I'm dying.

"Hang on. I'll go as fast as I can."

With her knees she gripped his hips. Her left arm looped round his shoulders and sometimes slipped against his neck.

"Sorry," Kelly mumbled.

"It's all right," Evan replied, coughing. "I know you've often wanted to throttle me, but I'm not sure this is the right moment."

"If you get us out of this, I promise I won't say another cross word – ever."

Evan stopped to get his breath back. "Can I have that in writing?"

"Yes, if you've got a piece of paper, a pen and a right arm you can lend me."

At first, it was a struggle to haul up himself and Kelly when there was a big gap between steel rods. It soon became a struggle even with the small gaps.

Much of her weight lay on his shoulders. His quivering arms and the backs of his legs ached. He seemed to be carrying the world on his back.

When he next stopped to gather strength, he yelled upwards, "Can you hear me?"

Sarah's voice drifted down, "Have you got her?"

"Yes. Sort of. She's in bad shape. Have you got a plank ready?"

"Nearly," Matt answered. "I've found a metal sheet that'll reach across."

"Good," Evan called. "Don't rest it on the top cable. Try and put it a few rungs down so I can climb above it."

"Why?"

"You'll be able to see us soon. Then you'll see why. I need to lower Kelly on to it. And I think you'll have to help her across it. Okay?"

"Yes," Matt boomed. "We'll get it into position now."

Evan lapsed into silence as he put all his effort into dragging himself and his sister up towards the light. At one point he heard a gasp from above. Sarah must have seen them. She was obviously startled but Evan was reassured. They must be near the top. It was certainly getting lighter and he thought it might also be colder and less damp, but he was too hot and sweaty to be sure. On his back, Kelly was weeping to herself. Between sobs, she muttered, "You know, Evan, I never told you before. You're some brother. Full of surprises. Hidden depths."

Panting, he replied, "I'm not doing this every day, you know."

She looked up and whispered, "I can see Sarah's face. She looks petrified. Not far to go."

"Just as well," he gasped. "I can't do much more."

Kelly sniffed and, through tears, said, "You can make it. I trust you."

His body was throbbing with exhaustion. Cramp threatened to grip his left leg but he hoped to reach fresh air first.

Kelly shifted her position a little and a stabbing pain in her right shoulder made her scream.

"Are you okay?" Evan said.

At the same time a voice – much closer now – called down, "What's happened?"

"It's all right," Kelly muttered. "I've just nobbled my shoulder as well, I think."

Matt's practical tones floated down to them. "Not far, just a few metres. Keep coming straight up, Evan, and the plate will be on your left."

"Good. As long as I don't come up and bang my head on it."

"No. I'll warn you if you drift underneath it. I'm on it now, ready to grab her."

"Okay," Evan replied, trying to keep moving slowly and steadily. Between wheezes he shouted,

"Keep clear of her right side. Broken arm – maybe shoulder as well."

He heaved on the next rod and planted his foot securely on another rung. He was so drained of energy that he wanted to be sick, yet his stomach felt tormentingly empty. He swallowed several times to try and get rid of the foul taste in his mouth and throat.

On his back, Kelly was barely conscious. "Kelly!" Evan yelled. "Don't drift off. You might let go." He coughed, then added, "If you fall back down again, I'm not coming to get you."

Kelly managed a brief, strained giggle. "Don't you love me any more? Or is it back-seat drivers that you can't stand?"

Evan moaned theatrically. Refreshed by Kelly's quip, he reached up and tugged.

A few minutes later, his head emerged from the hole and he saw Matt astride a steel plate on his left.

"Twist round a bit," Matt said, "and I'll take her. I can get her by her good side."

When the weight lifted from his shoulders and hips, Evan felt so light – so giddy and insecure – that he thought he would float away. He clung to the giant frame, unable to move.

Matt steered Kelly into her sister's arms and came back to pluck Evan off the skeleton of steel. As he guided Evan along the plate and back to solid ground, he said in total admiration, "That's the bravest thing I've ever seen."

From the ramp, another voice responded, "I agree. None of my chaps would be brave – or stupid – enough to try it."

It was Eric Henderson and he was wearing a green jumper and wielding a length of heavy iron pipe. He looked like a policeman with a truncheon.

15

Sarah reacted first. "You!" she cried, taking a step towards Henderson as if to protect the others. "We know all about you. We know why you killed Mum."

The builder looked askance at Sarah, took a step towards her and proclaimed, "You know why I'd have liked to get rid of your mum, that's all. I didn't kill her."

Sarah hesitated. She wasn't sure what to believe. He seemed to be irritated in the same way that she would be irritated by a false accusation, yet there was a lot of hard evidence against him. On top of everything, he'd thrown Kelly down a pit and left her for dead. She squared up to him. "You're lying," she said.

"Listen." He walked right up to her and spoke slowly and firmly. "I had nothing to do with your mother's death."

Sarah stared into his face and knew that he was telling the truth. The realization unnerved her. She opened her mouth to reply, but her lips couldn't form any words.

Matt stood by her side protectively. "But you disposed of the body," he said. "This business with Kelly proves it."

"Yes," he admitted. "I can hardly deny that."

"You know who killed her, don't you?" Matt retorted.

Eric Henderson nodded.

"We think we know too," Sarah told him.

Curious, he cocked his head on one side. "Oh?"

"Her."

"What? Who?"

Sarah pointed behind him. "Her. Your accomplice. Vicky McCormick."

The police officer had crept up quietly while they talked.

Henderson hesitated, not sure if Sarah was playing a trick on him. Then he spun round, holding the pipe high above his head, and brought it down sharply.

Vicky McCormick dived to one side but she wasn't fast enough. There was a sickening crack as the metal hit the side of her head and bounced on to her shoulder. A small moan issued from her mouth. She was unconscious by the time her body thudded into the mud.

"No!" Sarah screeched, staring in horror at Henderson. "How could you—"

Impatiently, he interrupted, "She must have followed you. Waiting in the wings, no doubt. She was letting you do the hard work, so don't feel sorry for her. Thought she'd just have to turn up at the end to grab the glory."

Matt knelt down beside the policewoman and felt her chest, neck and wrist. "I . . . er . . . I think she's dead."

Henderson simply shrugged.

Standing up and returning to Sarah's side, Matt remarked, "It wasn't her you were working with, then."

Mr Henderson grinned unpleasantly. "Her? You've got some strange notions in your heads. She's a cop." Still holding the bloodied metal tube, he declared, "Anyway, this is very convenient. I've got all the people who suspect me together in one place."

"You can't get rid of all of us," Sarah exclaimed. "You won't get away with it."

"We could run," Matt said. "At least one of us will get away."

Henderson laughed. "I can't see Kelly or Evan doing much running, and you two won't leave them."

From behind Sarah and Matt, Evan pushed himself upright and barked, "I can still run. Besides, it's all over for you. We've got a copy of a certain letter. It shows that you've been cutting corners with building materials. We've left it with a friend, as insurance. It goes to the police if we don't show up soon. And it makes you look as guilty as hell."

"You're bluffing."

"Does this sound familiar?" Evan asked. "Something along the lines of, 'We must point out that this aggregate is cheap because of its poor quality. Concrete made from it will fail impact tests.' Does it ring a bell? I think you know the letter. I'm not bluffing."

Mr Henderson glared at Evan for a few seconds, then relented. Reaching into a pocket, he pulled out a mobile phone. Still keeping an eye on his captives, he punched in a number and waited. Someone must have answered because he spoke. "It's me. We've got trouble." He listened to a reply, then said, "No, there's no choice. You'll have to come. Ring-road site. Take the track opposite Salt Lane. You can't miss us." He put the phone away and said, "The person you want will be here in ten minutes. For now, we stay here and talk. I have a little proposition for you."

"What do you mean?" asked Evan.

"I'll give you the killer on a plate – and the

evidence you need. In return, you give me the letter. That's the deal. Of course, you forget that Sergeant McCormick was ever here as well."

"Who is it and what's the evidence?" Matt demanded.

"Do we have a deal?"

Indignantly, Sarah snapped, "After what you've just done to Kelly!"

"I did try to warn her."

"You did?"

"I heard from . . . a certain person that you lot had been nosing around. I volunteered to warn you off. Didn't you tell them about the phone call?" Henderson directed his question over Sarah's shoulder to Kelly, who was still propped against the wooden structure.

Kelly shook her head. "No," she responded weakly. "I didn't tell them. Didn't want to frighten anyone."

"That's hardly the point," Sarah retorted. "If you had an ounce of good in you, you'd be calling for an ambulance right now. Kelly's in a terrible state."

"If we've got a deal, I'll call."

"And you want us just to forget Vicky McCormick? You're a monster!" Sarah walked back to her sister, muttering, "If it was just me, you wouldn't get a deal."

Matt felt like an intruder. He wasn't a Keating

and he didn't feel that he had the right to make or break any bargains. He kept his thoughts to himself. Kelly would have had an opinion but she was hardly capable of expressing it. They all looked at Evan.

"First, I've got a few questions," Evan said. Henderson was the one with the weapon, but Evan was in control. "How did you know we were here?"

"Some responsible citizen saw the floodlights. Thought it odd at this time. She took the telephone number from our hoarding and called to let me know. I was working late in the office," he explained. "I didn't believe that the rats had set off the security lights."

"What about George McCormick? You've been avoiding mentioning him."

"He's got nothing to do with us, here and now."

"So, you *did* kill him. Presumably because, once Mum's body was discovered, he realized you'd used sub-standard materials and murdered Mum because she threatened you. Tried to bribe you to stop work on the factory."

"You *have* got this notion about me firmly fixed in your brain, haven't you? As if I'm the only bad guy. No, I didn't kill him."

Evan wasn't so sure. Even if he hadn't murdered McCormick, he was certainly in on it, otherwise he would have claimed that Vicky's husband had committed suicide. "It's down to this . . . certain person again, then?"

"That's right," Henderson smirked. He reminded Evan of a naughty schoolboy who always managed to get someone else into trouble while avoiding the flak himself. "Okay, tell me why he killed Mum and McCormick," Evan continued.

Henderson's face crinkled. "Why? You want to know *why*, not *who*?"

Evan surprised everyone by announcing, "I know *who*, but I've no idea *why*. Has he just flipped his lid?"

"Just a minute," Sarah interjected. "Who are we talking about?"

Evan turned towards his sister. "Who – apart from Vicky McCormick – could have told him," he jabbed a thumb towards Mr Henderson, "that Kelly was on the warpath tonight, and where she'd be?"

From behind Sarah, Kelly's pained voice muttered "Daniel Perriman."

"Right," Evan responded.

Together, Sarah and Matt cried, "Perriman?"

Henderson watched them with some amusement on his face. He didn't spoil his fun by confirming or denying it. He simply listened.

"Who else could it be?" Evan argued. He turned to Eric Henderson and said, "You knew Mum was having an affair, didn't you? Must have heard it on the grapevine at work."

Henderson gave the merest nod. It was meant to encourage Evan to continue.

"But you didn't know who with, did you?"

"Bingo!" Henderson replied. His twisted smile looked like a black hole in his bushy beard.

Matt was puzzled. "What's that got to do with it?"

"Don't you see?" Evan said. "It explains why Perriman's description of the man in the restaurant was wrong, and why he identified McCormick later. It's all falling into place."

"You what?"

"Mum met Henderson that night, not McCormick." Evan ignored Henderson's sarcastic laugh. "It was a bit late in the day but Mum tried to blackmail him to abandon Mr Warr's extension, using the letter she must have just found. Apparently, she decided to tackle him away from the office – over a meal at the seafood place. Or maybe that was Henderson's idea. Anyway, between them Perriman and Henderson killed her and hid her body. They knew she had a lover, so they cooked up this story about her meeting her mystery man in the restaurant. But they didn't know who he was, so Perriman just gave a vague description of an imaginary diner. Told the police they looked like scheming lovers and, hey presto, Tatton put two and two together and came up with five, just like he was supposed to. Mum had run off with another man."

"So, there is a brain of sorts inside that head of yours," Eric Henderson sneered.

Evan turned back to him. "Bit risky, wasn't it?" he remarked. "You must have worried about what her boyfriend would do when he heard that he was supposed to have run off with her."

"Yes, but we had to take that risk. We reckoned that, if he was a married man, he'd probably say nothing. For all we knew there might have been more than one lover. Each would think she'd taken off with the other. It was a calculated gamble."

"But McCormick did crack it eventually. Made a nuisance of himself," Evan deduced, "probably by threatening to tell his wife that you had the motive to murder Mum. Or maybe he said he'd expose your bad workmanship and have you closed down. Either way, he had to go. By then it must have been obvious to you that he was the mysterious boyfriend."

Sarah joined in. "You and Perriman poisoned him and wrote that suicide note. The rejected lover story wrapped it up neatly. Inspector Tatton made two and two add up to five again," she concluded.

"Very good," Henderson scoffed.

"Yes," Evan muttered. "But why? I understand your motive, but why did Perriman kill Mum?"

"Ask him yourself." Henderson nodded his head in the direction of the track where a pair of headlights searched out the pot-holes and bumps. "But before he arrives, what about our deal?"

"What evidence are you offering that Perriman did it?"

"Do we have a deal?"

Evan glanced at the others. They were silent. It was up to him. To Sarah's relief, he pronounced, "No deal. You tried to kill Kelly. You've killed Vicky McCormick in front of our own eyes. At best, you're implicated in the murder of George McCormick and Mum. All to protect your second-rate building business. No deal."

Henderson sighed theatrically. "I'm very sorry about that. You'll be sorry too. You leave me no choice."

Daniel Perriman picked his way distastefully across the site, avoiding the tools and works vehicles. He looked like a worried man. Before he joined the small crowd, he hesitated, surveying the scene. He was trying to gauge the extent of the problem. The expression on his face suggested that he'd concluded it was a big one. He shook his head sadly, then trudged up to them and stood alongside Eric Henderson. "What's going on?" he inquired.

Henderson was brief. "They've worked it all out."

Kelly staggered forward and fixed Mr Perriman with her eyes. She asked, "Why did you kill her?"

"Is that what *he* told you?" He meant Henderson.

"That's what we've worked out for ourselves, and what he confirmed."

"I didn't kill her."

"What?" Sarah exploded as she helped to prop up her trembling sister.

"There's no one else," Evan reasoned. "It must have been you."

Perriman shrugged. The pressure on him was beginning to tell. "You might as well know the truth," he said. "I *didn't* kill her. Not really. No one did. She was the first customer to have a new batch of shrimps."

"Shrimps?"

"Yes. Shrimps. They . . . er . . . weren't good." Daniel Perriman seemed to be genuinely sorry, as well as afraid. "Have you ever heard of blue-green algae?" Without waiting for a reply from his stunned audience, he continued, "Apparently huge numbers of them suddenly grow, and shrimps graze on them. The trouble is—"

"Is this for real?" Sarah interrupted.

"Yes," Perriman replied with as much force as he could muster.

"Let him finish," Evan said. "I think I've seen a programme about this, or read about it. Blooms of algae. They're poisonous, aren't they?"

Mr Perriman bucked up on hearing Evan. He

took his comment as support. "Yes. The chemicals from the algae – they're called toxins – concentrate in shrimps. I had a load of Philippine shrimps. They were good value, but I didn't know then that they'd been collected when there was an algal bloom in the area. I checked afterwards and destroyed the remainder. It's not easy to monitor absolutely everything that I buy for the restaurant, you know; something as rare as this is easily overlooked. An amount the size of a pin-head can kill a human being. That's what did it," he concluded.

"That's horrible!" Sarah exclaimed. "You two just watched her die! Why didn't you do something, like call an ambulance?"

"She went very quickly," Mr Perriman said in his defence.

Henderson agreed. "One minute, she said she had a funny tingling in her lips. She didn't take it too seriously. Then she said she was going numb in the mouth. A few seconds later, she collapsed."

The restaurant owner took up the story. "She was paralysed by it. Couldn't swallow or breathe. That's what this toxin does. An ambulance couldn't have done anything for her, I'm afraid. It was all over in a couple of minutes. I would still have reported it, but *he* stopped me."

Henderson looked at his accuser sternly. "That's nonsense, and you know it. All I did was point out that we were both in the same boat. Cheap products had got the better of us. I had to use them or go bankrupt; you chose not to check your raw materials properly." Addressing Evan, he added, "You see, your mum was threatening my business, and a case of food poisoning would certainly have put paid to a restaurant's business. We were both against the ropes. You have to protect your livelihood. There's not a lot of hope if you go bust these days. So I just pointed out that it was in both our interests to cover up your mum's death, that's all. I didn't want the police sniffing round the building yard. And you," he said to Perriman, "didn't want them closing you down. We agreed it was for the best."

Mr Perriman gazed at the ground. "Yes, we agreed. But now it's getting out of hand."

"You both sorted out George McCormick when he twigged what was going on."

"Only because Henderson forced me," Perriman insisted. "He took me to McCormick's house, intent on setting up a suicide. He had it all planned. He said it was common knowledge that McCormick kept himself going with pills. We found bottles of the stuff in his bathroom. Henderson held him down and made me feed him the pills," Perriman snivelled. "A whole bottleful."

"How could you be forced to do that?"

Perriman glanced nervously at the builder, then

replied, "He said he'd take some evidence to the police if I didn't cooperate."

"Evidence?" Evan murmured. "I think it's time we heard about this evidence."

"My dinner guest died under my own nose," Henderson explained. "I put some of her uneaten meal in my pocket when *he* wasn't watching. Just in case it was the food and I needed a little . . . persuasion power. I've still got it in my freezer. I'm sure a decent forensic scientist would find traces of that toxin stuff in it. It gets me off the hook, that's for sure. And," he continued, talking to the restaurant owner, "it means you'll help me clear up the mess here and now."

"Clear up? What do you mean?"

"These," he said, indicating his four captives and the motionless policewoman, "are the loose ends that need tidying up."

"No!" Perriman objected. "It's gone too far. It went too far with McCormick. This is too much."

"Be careful what you say," Henderson growled. "You're a loose end as well."

"I . . . er . . ."

"Look. They won't run away because they won't leave Kelly. We can finish it right now. Don't you want to see the back of this affair? Remember your nice little business. Remember I've got the evidence on you."

"I don't know," Perriman dithered.

"Well," Matt said, "there's something else you both should think about. When I went to Vicky's body, I felt a police radio in her inside pocket. I turned it on. There's another loose end for you. And judging by the cars coming . . ." He pointed towards the track.

Perriman spun round but Henderson spluttered, "Don't be daft! He's bluffing. No sirens . . ."

Matt and Evan glanced at each other. Suddenly Evan knew that Matt was bluffing, but he also knew what he was thinking.

Catching Perriman off guard, Evan dived on him, pushing him violently into Henderson. The flailing piece of tubing crashed into the restaurant manager and not Evan. By the time Henderson was ready to strike again, Matt was behind him, pinning his arms to his chest in a bear hug.

"Hit him! Knock him out!" Matt screamed to Evan.

"But . . ." Evan had never hit anyone before.

"It's the only way!"

"No," Sarah said. "Use this."

She picked up a length of rope and offered it to Evan.

"No," Evan muttered to his sister. "You tie him. I'll help holding him. Just in case."

Swiftly, before he could be kicked, Evan ducked down and swept Henderson off his feet. Matt held down his top half and Evan took care of his legs while Sarah tied his hands behind his back, then coiled the rope round his ankles.

The three of them stood up and watched their victim writhing in the mud.

"He's not going anywhere," Matt declared, satisfied with the bonds.

"I know where I'd like to put him," Sarah mumbled, glancing towards the wooden frame.

"No," Kelly replied. "That's enough."

"Yes, I know really," Sarah muttered as she clung to Matt.

"What about you?" Evan said, standing over Mr Perriman, who was whimpering on the ground. "It's over, isn't it? You're not going to try anything, are you?"

If Perriman said anything, it was gibberish. He wasn't a threat. He was finished – a broken man.

"What do we do now?" asked Sarah.

From behind her, a voice spoke. "You help me to my car, so I can radio for assistance." Vicky McCormick, one side of her face covered in blood, was sitting up by the side of the ramp.

"But you're . . ." Sarah turned questioningly to Matt. "You said she was dead."

"I thought if I told him she was dead, he wouldn't hurt her any more. I also hoped she'd recover and come to our rescue, like the cavalry."

"Sorry," Vicky mumbled. "Better late than never, eh? But I do feel like I've risen from the dead." She tried to get to her feet but failed. "I'm dizzy," she said.

"You might have a fractured skull," Matt suggested.

"So, are you going to help me up?" she prompted.

With Evan on one side and Matt on the other, they dragged her up and across the site towards the car. Halfway there, Matt said, "I really don't know why I'm doing this, Evan. You could give her a piggy-back. After all your practising with Kelly, you'd be good at it."

Evan grinned weakly. "Very funny," he muttered.

Behind them, Sarah had linked arms with Kelly and together they watched over the helpless culprits. "Won't be long," Sarah said. "Soon get you fixed up in hospital."

"Yeah," her sister replied. "I think I need it." She rested her head on Sarah's shoulder and, through her sobs, said, "It's hurting, Sarah." She took a deep breath and added, "Actually, it's agony."

Sarah put a hand on Kelly's head. "I know. But at least it's all over."

Kelly tried to find a smile for her war-torn face. "Yeah. Knowing what happened, it's almost like getting Mum back. We can't really bring her back, but she's ours again. We've got a memory of her now."

"That's not all," Sarah replied. "I think we've regained a brother."

16

Thump! Thump! Thump! Thump!

Suddenly a cry went up behind him. "Evan!"

He spun round.

"You're wanted," the coach cried.

The Scorpion's first-choice forward was hobbling off the pitch on a damaged ankle and Evan was the only substitute who was a striker.

"Oh!" Evan left the practice football at the school wall and ran to the touch-line.

"Up front," the coach instructed him. "Straight swap for Colin. You've got ten minutes to show us what you can do, to show us you're a team player. A goal at this stage will finish the game, so get in there and do the business."

Evan ran tentatively on to the pitch, touching hands with Colin.

The coach turned to a spectator, the father of the goal-keeper, and whispered, "New lad. A bit young, but big for his age. A friend of Matt's. Didn't want to use him really. He's skilful on the ball but a loner. Keeps the ball to himself."

It took five minutes for Evan to warm to the pace of the game and settle into his position. Then, taking the ball from the half-way line, he dribbled expertly round three of the opposition.

"Pass it!" the coach screamed.

Evan ignored him, tangled with a defender and fell over.

"I knew it!" the coach muttered. "He's lost it."

Immediately, Evan scrambled back to his feet and, before the centre-back could get rid of the ball, took it off him again. The last defender was made of sterner stuff, though. He still couldn't separate Evan from the football but he forced him out wide to the right.

The coach buried his head in his hands. "Watch. He'll shoot from there," he groaned. "It's an impossible angle. Wasted chance."

Evan stopped and put his foot on the ball. He lined up for the shot. The defender rushed in to block it. Then, out of the blue, Evan dummied the shot, turned inside his marker and crossed the ball, chipping it over the keeper's head. The delay had given Matt, the Scorpion's big left back, time to charge upfield. No one else bothered. They thought they'd sussed out Evan's virtuoso style of play. It would be glory for him or, more likely, a lost opportunity for the team.

Matt leapt into the air and headed the ball down into the goal that was as open as the Scorpions' mouths.

Evan walked calmly back up the field ready for the centre while Matt shrugged off the congratulations of his mates. "Come off it," he said. "You saw who made the goal. Still think he's selfish, eh?" He ran up to Evan and slapped him on the back. "Now that's what I call a cross. Reckon you can do it again?"

Evan hesitated then smiled broadly. "I don't see why not."

On the touch-line, the coach was still trying to find his voice. At last he managed to murmur to his neighbour, "You've . . . er . . got to hand it to him. Perhaps he'll be a part of the team after all." Cupping his hands round his mouth, he yelled, "Great play, Evan! Now you've learned how to pass the ball, do it quicker next time."

Evan glanced back at Matt just before play resumed. The left back shrugged. "Never satisfied," he called to Evan.

In the small band of spectators, Sarah joined in the celebrations. It was her first football match and she hadn't got a clue about the rules of the game, but she knew a goal when she saw one, so she jumped up and down and shouted joyfully with everyone else. She wasn't just cheering the goal, made by her brother and scored by her boyfriend – she was rejoicing in Evan's return to the real world.

Back at home, the mood was more sombre. Kelly's dislocated shoulder had been put back in its proper place and the bone in the forearm had been set. She was still strapped like an Egyptian mummy and she was under doctor's orders to take it easy. No parties, no driving, no football matches, just rest. One hundred per cent boredom.

While the others were at the match, she went upstairs to investigate the bumps and bangs coming from her dad's room.

Her father was kneeling in his bedroom, surrounded by all manner of odds and ends. Kelly noticed the briefcase, jewellery box, and lots of her mother's clothes among the big heap of things on his bed.

"What are you doing, Dad?" she asked.

"Ah, Kelly. It's . . . I thought it was time to have a clear out."

Kelly nodded slowly and smiled at him. "Yes," she agreed. "I think you're right."

He got up and hugged his daughter briefly. "Thanks for telling me what really happened. I didn't realize how much I needed to know till you told me."

Kelly had hated every moment of the telling but she knew all along that she'd have to describe her mother's death. She'd picked the right moment – just after he'd driven her back from the hospital – and told him everything. Every messy detail. He had to know it all if he was going to come to terms with her death and learn to live without her.

Now, tears came easily to his eyes. "I knew all along she was seeing another man, but I shut it out of my mind. I just couldn't admit it." He wiped his eyes and exhaled. "Anyway, she's certainly not coming back, so it's no use keeping all her things. I phoned a charity that collects this sort of stuff. They'll be round later today. They're welcome to it."

"Good idea," Kelly replied. She didn't offer to help. She believed that her dad needed to do it himself. It was his therapy.

The police found the remains of the shrimp salad in Eric Henderson's freezer. The food and its toxin had not deteriorated, and analysis confirmed that the shrimps had been polluted by blue-green algae. It was a lethal salad.

The forensic evidence was interesting but unnecessary.

When Kelly had gone out that night to meet Detective Sergeant McCormick, she'd taken a small cassette recorder in her pocket, intending to tape their conversation. During the confrontation with Henderson, she'd managed to slip the recorder into Evan's hand, and Evan had moved close enough to Henderson and Perriman to get the whole conversation on tape. In police interviews, Perriman's silence and Henderson's wriggling were to no avail. Evan had already supplied the police with everything they needed.

Patched up and back at work, Vicky McCormick oversaw both prosecutions. As Henderson had predicted, she grabbed the glory. And that wasn't her only success. Through the post she received a photograph of a young man. On the back someone had written, "Pete. Runs gambling racket for kids. Revolvers." The information allowed her to wind up an unsavoury trade that had got many youngsters into trouble. When the Superintendent queried her source and excellent rate of success, she replied, "Having the right connections is one of the hallmarks of a good detective, isn't it, sir?"

The luckless Chief Inspector Tatton was moved to a different section and Vicky was promoted into his job. She had a lot to thank the Keatings for.

The extension to the video factory was declared unsafe. With Mr Warr in no position to argue, in case someone should spill the beans on the unlawful part of his enterprise, the wall at the bottom of the Keatings' garden was demolished and the view from the back of the house was restored. It wasn't the prettiest of scenes but it was a lot better than a lump of concrete.

Barbara Keating would have approved.

Don't miss these gripping Point Crime
mysteries available wherever you buy books,
or use the order form below.

Don't miss these great P•INT CRIME mysteries!

THRILLERS